# THE WARAL CODE

# THE WARAL CODE

## A BOTANICAL THRILLER

MARTY STONE

gatekeeper press
Where Authors are Family™

Columbus, Ohio

The Waral Code: a botanical thriller

Published by Gatekeeper Press
2167 Stringtown Rd, Suite 109
Columbus, OH 43123-2989
www.GatekeeperPress.com



Library of Congress Control Number: 2021950686

ISBN (paperback): 9781662922893
eISBN: 9781662922909

# Contents

**I Germination: . . . . . . . . . . . . . . . . 11**

1 A Waral without compassion is no Waral at all. 16

2 The Warals do not depend on deities nor regality. . . . . . . . . . . . . . . . . . . . . . . . . . 18

3 To be a reasonable and a responsible Waral is not an easy task. . . . . . . . . . . . . . . . . . . 19

4 To study as many cultures as possible and to study theological teachings will allow a Waral to navigate between them, peacefully. . . . . . . 21

5 Discussion and respect are an essential part of the Waral way of life. . . . . . . . . . . . . . . 23

6 The Waral way of life honours the links between the natural and the mechanical world. . 24

7 A Waral's education never stops. . . . . . . . . 25

8 The Waral way of life is not just an ethical and natural philosophy, it must be regarded as much more; it is a lifestyle and an ideal. . . . . . 26

9 Any citizen of the world may choose to become a Waral. . . . . . . . . . . . . . . . . . . 27

10 Any lady, gentlemen or other who has attained majority may choose to become a Waral. . . . . . . . . . . . . . . . . . . . . . . . . . 28

11 The Waral way of life stands between the constraints of Chelone and the strict rule of the Dragoons. . . . . . . . . . . . . . . . . . . . . 29

12 The Warals recognise that humanity serves nature, not the other way around. . . . . . . . . 30

13 The Warals travel with the essential bloom wherever they go. . . . . . . . . . . . . . . . . . . 32

**II Growth and nutrition: . . . . . . . . . . 35**

14 Any Waral has the authority to build a new Sanctuary. . . . . . . . . . . . . . . . . . . . . . 44

15 No Waral is born a Waral. To attain Warality is a choice; it is neither hereditary nor can it be imposed on anyone. . . . . . . . . . . . . . . . . 51

16 Warality is a Waral's peace of mind as well as a Waral's piece of mind. . . . . . . . . . . . . . 52

17 The most important law of the Waral way of life is: One law, One love. . . . . . . . . . . . . . 59

18 Warality is the embodiment of life, levity, prosperity, connectivity, respectability, diversity and responsibility. . . . . . . . . . . . . 64

19 A Waral's Summon and the rituals accompanying it can be performed privately although to share them is not uncommon. . . . . 71

20 One becomes a Waral when referred to as such by another person. Not a moment before. . 75

21 Those who are learning the Waral way of life but that have not attained the title of Waral are known as Hatchlings. . . . . . . . . . . . . . . . 79

**III Propagation: . . . . . . . . . . . . . 89**

22 A Waral may be given or choose many totems or signs. But only one will give away its secrets to a Waral. . . . . . . . . . . . . . . . . . 98

23 The Waral way is absolutely against prejudice and discrimination. . . . . . . . . . . 102

24 A Waral must honour the laws of land upon which this Waral stands and roam. . . . . . . . 110

25 Warals do not seek fame nor fortune, they seek wisdom. . . . . . . . . . . . . . . . . . . 116

26 One of a Waral's many roles is to preserve and protect humanity's natural and cultural heritage. . . . . . . . . . . . . . . . . . . . . . 119

27 The Warals acknowledge that conflict is sometimes inevitable, but violence must never be used as a resolution for said conflicts. . . . . 121

28 Totems and signs are only artefacts to help a Waral focus. They are the basis for a well conducted ritual, but they are not necessary. . 125

29 Totems and signs do not possess any powers, they are only self-motivational tools. . 130

30 A Waral must share the history of the Waral way of life. . . . . . . . . . . . . . . . . . . . 131

**IV Admixture: . . . . . . . . . . . . . . 137**

31 A true Waral is constantly learning and teaching. . . . . . . . . . . . . . . . . . . . . 153

32 Following the Waral way of life and stepping into a sanctuary is a choice. . . . . . . . . . . 155

33 The Warals acknowledge the natural and organic recycling process of life and death. They recognise that life and death are two different sides of the same process of existence. . . . . . . . . . . . . . . . . . . . . 156

34 Each Waral who decides to make use of the essential bloom must make it bloom personally unless physically unable to do so. . 158

35 The Warals honour both the wrath and the generosity of Ferika. They regard Ferika as both the mother of modern mankind and the motherland of mankind. . . . . . . . . . . . . . 160

36 The Warals must assist any person in need. 164

37 Any Waral inviting visitors in a sanctuary must be responsible for said visitors. . . . . . 165

38 A Waral sanctuary is open to any visitor, hatchling and Waral. . . . . . . . . . . . . . . . 167

39 The Waral way of life regards that the respect and worship of nature is natural indeed. 171

40 The Warals believe in the cycle of life and death that is existence and they serve nature. . 174

41 To attain Warality one must go through three distinct phases; a vision, a walkabout and finally a phase of construction. . . . . . . 176

42 (the latest article) The Warals acknowledge that humanity has a rare gift; introgression. . . 178

**V Introgression: . . . . . . . . . . . . . . 181**

*Letter to Sister O', resident of the Sanctuary de la Chocolatine, Northern New Gaul. From Professor Simon I. Harding, Derwood, Maryland, North America (year Alpha six point zero).*

*I regret to inform you that your little Orange miracle, my dear friend Noël Joseph, has been missing for the past five weeks. He was declared dead this morning. Please accept my condolences. I am and always will be there for you. You know how to reach me directly or through the agency if you choose to do so.*

*Shortly before his disappearance, Noël asked me to help him translate his book; the Waral code. He specifically entrusted me to send you a copy. My old friend wanted you to be the first to read his precious code. As you know, he spent years of his life traveling around the globe in search of clues related to the history of the followers of the Waral way of life. Their secretive lifestyle has always fascinated him. In this parcel, you will find Noël's precious manuscript, accompanied by passages from my personal accounts for you to read.*

*Noël wanted you to know that he loved you very much. You were always like a mother to him.*

*I am so sorry for your loss,*
*Simon "Sam" I. Harding.*

# I Germination:

Les and I are glad that the head of the Earthican Council is still in charge of preserving peace around the world. The new administration is dedicated to honour the Earthican Accords. Heads of states, presidents and leaders of the world no longer wage war against each other. They finally realised that lies, bribery, genocide and ecocide are no longer considered profitable options. Communication systems and the media coverage are even faster than ever before; it is pretty impressive. In short, information can no longer hide! Unfortunately, our world is not as peaceful as it sounds. The Natural Liberation Front is still hiding in the natural zones, raiding defenceless populations and claiming lives. The Mechanic Revolutionaries, on the other hand, are still orbiting the globe in their sophisticated stations. They are becoming more dangerous than before. With the help of their long-distance armament, the Mechanics have managed to destroy New York City, London, Tokyo and Rio. Each passing year these high-tech Revolutionaries are bombing a different city while the Natural Front is still torturing hostages like the savages that they have become. The two extremist groups are no longer isolated parties. The media has labeled them as notoriously brutal organisations and every single one of their attacks makes the headlines on the news. I am glad that our agency, the Anti Bioterrorism and Bio-threat Agency, nicknamed A. B. B. A. by the general population, has finally been recognised as a global security asset. Just a couple of years ago A. B. B. A. got the approval to build the Delivery Station Laboratory by the Earthican Council. The Delivery Station, a massive self-sustaining drone acts as our independent laboratory. With this drone, we can finally contain and eradicate any bio-threat that presents itself, at least this is what the drone laboratory is supposed to do anyway. We also use this drone as a delivery service and rescuing piece of equipment. The Delivery Station contains multiple workshops, living quarters and a fully self-sustaining kitchenette. After showcasing the newly built Delivery Station to the Earthican Council, my old friend Noël, his then-girlfriend Judith and I decided to spend the weekend in the countryside. Professor Lou Walesky, Judith's father and Noël's former mentor, had invited us for a celebratory spring weekend in his farmhouse near Arras in Northern New Gaul. After re-uniting with Professor Walesky we partied all night. Professor Lou and his old hippy friends had already started the festivities. Even Dave, his crazy musician neighbour, was attending the party. Dave was acting stranger than usual that night. The young man was shrieking and flapping his arms in the air like a mad man. When noticing this perturbing spectacle, Lou informed us that Dave was just pretending to be a bat for the evening and that we should not pay much attention. Indeed, the young man was trying to communicate with what appeared to be a series of high-pitched ultrasounds. The evening was full of joy, full of smokable and full of booze. That evening, I drank and smoked like puffer fish. I can vividly remember the terror I felt the next morning when I received that faithful phone call. It was still early in the morning and I was barely emerging from a painful and foggy dream. A hangover was hovering around me and a serious headache dragged me out of the arms of Orpheus. Judith was shouting at me, she handed me the phone:

"Sam! Wake the fuck up, it's an emergency! You need to take this right now!"

"Okay luv', gimme a mo'." I replied." I am not a spring chicken anymore you know." I had to wake up. I grabbed the phone: "Simon I. Harding speaking, how may I assist y..." I could not finish.

Les was on the other line screaming, he was describing a scene of panic and disarray: "Sam! You and Noël need to get your asses down to Paris immediately! We got a serious situation on our hands, there is a plant releasing a toxic compound in the air. It is spreading fast and it is causing mass hysteria, police altercations and destruction of historical sites. I'm on my way aboard the Delivery Station with the team. Our first targeted area is in the Louis XVI Park. You and Nöel need to meet us there asap!"

"Roger that, dear", I replied, "we will be there in about two hours..."

"You'll have to do better than that!" said Les and he hung up right before I did.

We drove down to Paris as fast as we could to meet with our team near the Louis XVI Park located on the prestigious Haussmann Boulevard. Before going into any further details about this puzzling incident, I must admit how much our team is loyal and incredibly gifted.

Alice "Zed" Turing, twenty-nine, is an extraordinary talented young American bioengineer. She loves nature, particularly big cats. She has a passion for late 20th century "new metal" music. She calls the delivery station her home. Her bedroom is sitting above the backup motor on the first floor of our laboratory/ drone. She has been living and working aboard the delivery station since its original construction. Zed practically never steps away from her laboratory; she is a real workaholic. Seriously, she needs to spend more time outdoors. The young vibrant woman is as pale as a ghost. With her long white dreadlocks and her dark gothic outfits she can sometimes be a tiny bit intimidating. At times she may appear a bit rude, but deep down she has a good heart.

Mehdi Heffaz Cohen is in his late forties. He is a tall, tanned and suave gentleman. He is a brilliant French botanist and world-renowned translator. He has a particular interest in ancient Persian history. He knows how to play the Saz, the bouzouki, the lute and virtually everything with strings on it. Mehdi told us that he has been playing music since he was four years old. He learned how to speak sixteen languages, obtained a PHD in linguistics and became a medical assistant in the military before he turned thirty. This multi-talented genius was vigorously recommended to us by General Roken, our chief of security.

Dr. Margaret Burlington is a virologist and an accomplished engineer. She used to be part of the coleoptera robotic intervention project. She looks like your typical granny with her gigantic glasses and especially when she wears her light pink sweater. The woman is a pioneer in bio-threat prevention and has a background in general organic behaviours. She was born in South Africa, but she grew up in the animated neighbourhood of Adams Morgan in Washington D.C. Her younger brother Baggy has a company established somewhere in the Mongolian plateau. I believe that the two are still in good terms. Margaret's grandchildren call her "Mammy kitty" because she loves cats and collects cat memorabilia. Dr. Margaret Burlington and Zed often spend hours talking about felines, a subject that frankly bores me to tears. Among the members of the agency, Margaret Burlington is known as "Babs". Noël always thought of her as the funniest colleague we've ever had.

Lesley, "Les" D. Roken, is a former USAir force pilot and a retired general with an impeccable reputation. He is responsible for our security team. He was born on a secret military base on a remote US Island in the middle of the Pacific. After a while his family settled in North America, somewhere in West Virginia. Les has traveled around the globe at least sixteen times. He is the best cook I have ever met! He earned the title "#1 African-American chef" from the Black Enterprise Journal a few years back. The man is solid as a rock. Even at the age of sixty-seven he still spends hours running and working out every week. An accomplished defence and coordination expert, Les oversees logistics, security and a little bit more.

Noël Joseph is not just my business partner and the co-owner of the Agency, he is also a bright anthropologist, archeologist, sociologist, a distinguished historian, an invasive species expert and most importantly, my childhood friend. I remember when we met at the prestigious Bilingual School of Paris over fifty years ago. Back then, the other pupils mocked his Belgian accent and they used to call him the "orphan of Belgicca", but Noël did not mind. I will always remember how, with his long ginger frizzy hair and his tall and slinky stature, he looked like a thin paint brush dipped in bright orange paint.

And finally, yours truly, Simon "Sam" Israël Harding, botanist, virologist and head of the Anti-Bioterrorism and Bio-threat Agency. Back in that wretched school, I was known as the fat hobbit, due to my exquisitely thick Irish accent and my incredibly beautiful love handles. The students constantly called me Sam instead of Simon and, to my advantage, the name stuck.

We finally arrived in Paris to meet up with the team. Noël Joseph and I were on a new mission. We had lost our youth, but we had a new target to neutralise. We still had vigour pulsing through our veins. We were determined to eradicate this new organic target. My old friend Noël and I were ready to get to work.

## 1 A WARAL WITHOUT COMPASSION IS NO WARAL AT ALL.

Ancient myth from "The Recitations of the elders". Tombstone engraved by the first Grey scribe, on burial ground at the Murals and Legends museum in Remektpe, Northern Africa. (Partial tombstone still in place dating from around 9000 BC)

How the Warals got their name:

It is said that over one hundred thousand years ago, a group of nomads composed of multiple tribes travelled the land. They traveled with their respective cultures. They had different beliefs and some had non at all. They fled their home villages ravaged by the recent stone massacres. They had nowhere to go. The recent rise of the rule of the Dragoons had treated these different tribes like cattle and a simple workforce and in some instances as human shields. The ancient civilisation of Chelone had led these tribes to become nomads, the Chelonians had led them astray. The nomads traveled with the seasons along with their families. Some of them had seen Ferika, some remembered the sweet smell of knowledge of the serpentine city of Chelone. All the nomads had a peculiar gift; they knew how to read and communicate with their natural surroundings. Their name was to be given by a surprising ally.

One day the travellers needed to cross a river in search of more hospitable land. The water was welcoming and calm. One of the children approached the edge of the river when suddenly a monitor lizard slithered from the shore towards the land, scaring the child away from the river. A second child approached the water and another monitor lizard scared the child away. Before a third child decided to reach the water, the parents of the child noticed an enormous crocodile submerged in the murky river. They immediately pulled the child to safety. The parents alerted the rest of the group of nomads and warned them about the crocodile hiding beneath the surface of the water. The travellers realised what had just happened before their eyes. The monitors were trying to warn and scare the children away in order to expose the dangerous predator in the river. The nomads had no choice but to wait for the crocodile to go away. Later that day, one of the monitor lizards stood up on his hind legs and rested upwards with the help of its strong tail. The animal looked at the river, looked at the nomads and finally ran towards the river and swam across it. Soon after, a second monitor lizard ran toward the river and swam across it. The nomad understood that it was then safe to cross the waters and they did. Once on the other side of the bank, one of the nomads spotted a second group of nomads in the distance. This second group was, in turn, about to cross the river. All the children from the first group shouted:

"Careful! They are crocodiles in this river! Do not cross the river yet! Wait for the monitor lizards' warnings. They will tell you when it is safe to cross the river. Wait for the monitors' warning!"

On the other side of the river, the second group of nomads could only distinguish two words; warning and monitor lizards. These two words, coincidently, sounded almost the same for this second group of travellers. All they could hear from the other side of the river was a group of children shouting:

"Waral! Waral! Waral!".

These words were strong enough to convince the second group of nomads to look for the monitor lizards' warnings before crossing the river. And this is how these wise travellers adopted the name Warals to identify themselves. The Warals became the name of all of those who desired to remain independent of the rule of the Dragoons and the interminable constraints of the civilisation of Chelone. Since that faithful day, they adopted a very powerful saying: a Waral without compassion is no Waral at all.

## 2 THE WARALS DO NOT DEPEND ON DEITIES NOR REGALITY.

Ngea's legends inscribed on a decorative tablet, engraved by the first Anonymous scribe. Original artefact privately own, stored in an undisclosed location in Uet, Western Africa. (Tablet dating from around 5000 BC to 4500 BC)

The four elements of truth:

One of the first elders was one of the wisest teachers. This instructor, a Waral teacher, was respected by all. This wise teacher instructed all those seeking knowledge and education. This elder was often confronted to censorship from the theological constraints of Chelone and had suffered persecution from the regal rule of the Dragoons. This instructor was passing on philosophical and natural thoughts to all students seeking knowledge outside the realm of deities and regality. For the Warals do not depend on deities nor royalty; they think for themselves. This Warals' thoughts always revolved around the four natural elements of truth:

Water is the essence of life. Water is both creator and destroyer; water always has the last laugh.

Air is light, but never underestimate its power.

The Earth is our mother; she can and will always be both vengeful and rewarding.

Fire has the ability to dance for one just as well as for one hundred thousand. Never mistreat fire; for it can kill you as much as it can keep you alive.

One oral legend remains to this day surrounding the mysterious life of this instructor. It is said that this instructor never really died.

## 3 TO BE A REASONABLE AND A RESPONSIBLE WARAL IS NOT AN EASY TASK.

Passage from the tablets of Gmefke. Copied and distributed by the first Blue scribe, date unknown. Artefact privately owned and stored in an undisclosed location near Malinas, South America. (Tablet dating from around 2500 BC)

From Chelone to Dragoon, the origins of the Waral way of life:

According to ancient Waral legends, the world hatched from a single egg. Another legend states that a giant tortoise was the keeper of our world before it hatched from a single spec of life. The legend of the first egg is only a metaphor to illustrate the power of even the smallest of all specs of life. The Warals have always known that life as we know it is composed of a multitude of small specs intertwined with each other to form larger forms of lives. Today the followers of the Waral way of life do not follow spirits nor do they follow the orders imposed by the chiefs. The Warals only answer to the laws of nature. And while the rest of humanity is determined to tame the natural world, the followers of the Waral way of life, on the contrary, acknowledge that it is the natural world that has tamed humanity. This Waral philosophy had been frowned upon for thousands of years but the Warals did not care. They lived peacefully as they pleased and in the beginning they kept their knowledge to themselves.

Long before the royal rule of the Dragoons, there was a never-ending city,The City of Chelone. This civilisation was continually expanding under the supervision of a Council composed of ordinary Chelonians.

The city of Chelone and its civilisation grew. It crossed the deserts, the rivers, then the seas and finally distant and hostile lands. The serpentine city had become a massive collection of intertwined communities spread all over distant lands.

As the Chelonian civilisation expanded, it accumulated different customs, different beliefs and varying individuals coming from different localities. All these different ways and cultures managed to coexist as a strong unit for millennia.

A hundred thousand years ago the world of Chelone was dismantled, its citizens dispersed across the land, adopting new and foreign customs and cultures along the way. The Chelonians soon became foreigners to one an other.

The civilisation of Chelone was crying and calling for unity. Ferika answered the cries of the remaining Chelonians and she restored their civilisation. But this admirable feat did come at a terrible cost. Saving the ancient civilisation gave rise to the rule of the domineering Dragoons thirst for conquest.

The Waral did not follow the orders dictated by the spiritual leaders of Chelone, nor did they follow the dictates commanded by the Dragoons and their regal ambitions. The Warals followed their own path, a sophisticated path built on science, artistic prowess, responsibility and compassion. The followers of the Waral way of life respected and understood the beliefs of each and every citizen of the world. They quickly developed a moral obligation to stay out of the affairs of Chelone and away from the brutal ambitions of the newly established rule of the Dragoons.

As the Chelonians focused on preserving their history and their ancient mythology, the Dragoons, on the other hand, took pleasure in trying to dominate and drive the future. The Dragoons had a passion for exploitation and domination, using a series of authoritarian methods and deeply spiritual ideologies. They wanted to have a direct impact on their subjects' future actions. Since then, the Warals have been forced to navigate between the civilisation of Chelone and the Dragoon dominions in order to survive.

Ferika the first, or Ferika tout court, is recognised by the Warals as a historical figure and a mythical legend. She is regarded as the mother of modern mankind. It is said that she managed to unite all ancient humans of the lands and to persuade them to merge into one single form, notably us; modern humans. Ancient humans no longer roam the lands, neither do the elemental, nor the primordial, nor the Wilders, nor the giants and nor the elders. The Warals believe that despite the fact that ancient humans may no longer be with us or walk with us, their moral and organic heritage still remains within us to this day.

The followers of the Waral way of life are always well trained and prepared, but they remain peaceful. They truly believe that to be a reasonable Waral is not an easy task. They seek liberty and responsibility. Not only for themselves but they wish it for all inhabitants of the land, independently of their potential Chelonian attachments or their Dragoon beliefs.

## 4 TO STUDY AS MANY CULTURES AS POSSIBLE AND TO STUDY THEOLOGICAL TEACHINGS WILL ALLOW A WARAL TO NAVIGATE BETWEEN THEM, PEACEFULLY.

The scrolls of Rekrosotapolis, assembled by the first Red Scribe. On display at the Natural History Museum in Hyo Jeng, Indonesian Isles. (Artefact dating from around 600BC)

The cycle of an old cricket...

Xia was an intelligent and loyal disciple of the wisest of the elders of the land. But Xia wanted to discern the exact moment when life turned into death. This subject was taboo among the Chelonians and the Dragoons, but not for the Warals. Because for them, to study as many cultures as possible and to study theological teachings will allow a Waral to navigate between them, peacefully. The Warals appreciate the value of different points of view. Xia was determined and had to step away from the constraints of Chelone. Could animation and inanition be linked to the point of overlaps? Xia studied the question for a long number of years. Xia was forced to travel the world in search of different stories to answer the ultimate question concerning the cycle of life and death. The concept of transformation from one state, life, into another, death, was present in almost every culture, no matter the locality, the heritage or the theological beliefs. This transformation was for most inhabitants of the world, something more than a scientific process. But Xia had to use tact, respect and courtesy in order to get access to as many stories as possible. And from as many different sources as possible. One day Xia heard an ancient Waral story; there once was an old cricket and it could no longer eat. It could no longer move and passed away. The ants and the flies celebrated the departure of the cricket. They celebrated the cricket's natural rite of passage; re-distribution. Soon a banquet followed, all the tiny insects fed on the carcass of the cricket. After the feast the insects returned to their usual constructive activities and other sexual parades. In turn, mushrooms and a cluster of fungus cleaned the remains left by insects and the old cricket was no more. The well-fed insects reproduced, the mushrooms spread and the fungus flourished. All this activity lead to an accumulation of residues and moisture, just enough to allow a seed to grow into a tall grass. This tall grass was to become a banquet itself. A season passed and the tall grass bloomed. One morning, a different cricket ate the flowers, all of them. This cricket was growing old, it had no idea that this flowering blade of grass was to be its last meal. Eventually this old cricket passed away and new insects celebrated its departure... the cycle was completed, it was to re commence. Xia was never able to answer why death was an essential part of life nor why life was an essential part of death. But Xia was able to explore and determine the reason how this life circle was to endure for the rest of times. Xia was convinced that life and death were are not separate events. Many stories supported this extravagant theory. Zia had come to realise that life and death are simply different definitions of the natural process the Warals call existence.

## 5 DISCUSSION AND RESPECT ARE AN ESSENTIAL PART OF THE WARAL WAY OF LIFE.

Tales of Mi, partial cylinder translated and distributed by the first Orange scribe. Passage from the tablets bearing the same name, preserved at the Sanctuary of Weleem, Central Persia. (Relic dating from around 500BC.)

Chelone was tired...

Long after the emergence of Ferika, the creation of Chelone and the birth of the rule of the Dragoons, Mi, the combative, retuned home on the outskirts of the Chelonian civilisation. After a brush with death, witnessing conquests and destruction, Mi had a sudden realisation that being tired and tired of being are two different desires. The first was a natural option, while the second was most unnatural, indeed. Mi did survive the wars, adapted to the destructions imposed by external forces and eventually developed a stronger sense of commitment, passion and happiness. Mi was eventually able to overcome adversity and decided to remain independent from the rule of the Dragoons as well as the constraints of Chelone. Mi was a becoming Waral and a proud Waral. Mi requested and obtained liberty, acceptance and wished the same for all Earthicans, even for those rooting for the traditions of Chelone as well as the Dragoon sympathisers. Mi had been in contact with the enemies of Chelone as well as the enemies of the Dragoons. Mi had no choice but to regard each individual with love and respect. Discussion and respect were essential parts of the life of Mi, the combative Waral. Mi requested autonomy and obtained it by the means of tasteful discussions.

## 6 THE WARAL WAY OF LIFE HONOURS THE LINKS BETWEEN THE NATURAL AND THE MECHANICAL WORLD.

Passage from Mekbe's mémoires, translated and distributed by the first Golden scribe. Original artefact stored at the anthropology and sociology museum of little Bërn, Eastern New Gaul. (Mémoires dating from around 300 BC.)

The forest and the drum...

The forest had but one desire; it wanted to learn how to sing. The Warals had but one desire; they wanted to keep warm. The forest, sensitive to the Warals urgency whispered:

"Use my wood to keep warm, keep my leaves to build a shelter, keep my flowers as medicine and eat my fruits to keep fed. But please remember my roots and teach me how to sing."

The Warals listened to the wise advice and replied:

"We honour the links between the natural and the mechanical world, therefore, we will do as you command. We will remember your roots and honour you request. We will preserve your largest trunks and we will carve them into drums. We promise to make you sing through the end of times.

### 7 A WARAL'S EDUCATION NEVER STOPS.

Dlemius accounts of Sio's findings. Translated and distributed by the first Purple scribe. Ancient scrolls privately own in an undisclosed location in western Asia. (Scrolls dating from around 225BC.)

Where there are no snakes, lizards bite...

What else could be out there? Wondered Sio. Sio's only obsession was to catalog all mystical creatures of the Earth. Only the dragon posed a problem. After all, the African rooster and Gaulish cockerel still roamed the land. The lion's territory once extended further than the land of Ferika. The Persian raptors and the eagles of the distant lands still retained their original form. The serpents, the salamanders and the monitor lizards also held an important place in some hearts. The giants, the elementals, the primordials, the Wilders and all mystical creatures, even the sphinx appeared to be an integral part of nature. But the dragon imagery was a different historical and political animal. What was its origin? What was its purpose? Sio's investigation was impossible to stop. Perhaps to understand the dragon's nature one had to dismantle the myths and imageries surrounding it. Most of the dragon's imagery seemed to have originated with myths and legends surrounding lizards like monitors, tejus, flying agamas and diverse reptilian species. This theory was not far from the truth. Sio went on to travel around the world. During one of many voyages, Sio met a group of Warals. The Warals told Sio their stories and accounts surrounding the desire of the Dargoon rulers. This desire was to resemble their imaginary symbol, their totem: the mighty and untameable dragon. The domineering behaviour of the

Dragoons forced them to look upon a sacred mystical creature. The dragon was to become the Dragoons' coat of arms. The flying reptilian creature had the basic form of a lizard to represent control over the Warals. The creature's wings represented the total detachment of the civilisation of Chelone. This totemic figure had the ability to spit fire, acid or venom, depending on the sources. Some dragons had wings and four legs, others had two wings and two legs, some of them didn't have wings at all as to expressly represent a total detachment form the civilisation of Chelone. The totalitarian rule of the Dragoons and their favourite creature had no shame and no remorse. The dragon was a very effective symbol of regality, domination and refutation of the natural world, more so, than the salamander, the lion or any other creature of this land. When Sio finally returned home to divulge these recent discoveries, the local Emperor sentenced Sio to death for daring to criticise the majestic creature present on the imperial coat of arms. Sio's last words were: a Waral's education never stops. Sio's descendants never forgot and published the findings years later. We are grateful for the efforts and the sacrifice of Sio. Sio stories and accounts must not be forgotten.

## 8 THE WARAL WAY OF LIFE IS NOT JUST AN ETHICAL AND NATURAL PHILOSOPHY, IT MUST BE REGARDED AS MUCH MORE; IT IS A LIFESTYLE AND AN IDEAL.

Wailmoardi's diary, discovered, translated and distributed in 39 BC by the second Anonymous scribe. Passage quoting the book entitled "The pilgrim of time". Diary on display at the humanity museum of Rokyho, Western Eurasia. (Original manuscript dating from 74 BC)

Localities…

There once was a traveling pilgrim. He had seen many places, encountered all the different tribes of the lands, had studied all the local tales. This pilgrim had encountered Chelonians adventuring themselves out of the serpentine civilisation. He had also crossed the path of Dragoons on their way to war. One day the pilgrim stopped at a Waral sanctuary. The pilgrim was ageing fast; his health deteriorated rapidly. Despite all his travels and adventures, despite sharing half of his life with different populations, each having their own culture, each having their different local attribute, each having their different customs, the pilgrim wanted to know how many races of humans inhabited the world. When the pilgrim asked the wise Waral instructors about the number of human races inhabiting the lands, he was shocked and yet pleased by the answer he received; "There are no different races, for humanity is one gigantic family. The only race that concerns us is the race, the race against time."

The pilgrim soon discovered that what is known to us today as the Waral way of life is not just an ethical and a natural philosophy, it is an ideal. The pilgrim realised that the Warals did not believe in different human races. They viewed humanity as one single united species inhabiting different localities, nothing more, nothing less.

## 9 ANY CITIZEN OF THE WORLD MAY CHOOSE TO BECOME A WARAL.

Eomumi accounts of her father Deomum, translated and distributed by the Tranquil scribe. Partial manuscript privately owned in an undisclosed location in the Mediterranean basin. (Manuscript dating from 144 AD)

The land of Ferika:

Deomum was asked to trace a map of what was once known as the land of Alkebulan, also known as the land under the control of Africanus. The man was not sure how to properly name the map of this extraordinary land. Should this map be named after its inhabitants? Or should it be named after its government? One day, Deomum was asked to join a conversation with a group of followers of the Waral way of life. They invited the cartographer to join them as they believed that any citizen of the world may choose to become a Waral, or at least learn about their extraordinary path. Deomum discovered that this land was known to the Warals as A' Ferika, the land of Ferika. The legend tells us that the most complete map of Ferika was traced by Deomum, but it has never been delivered. It is believed that it is still waiting to be discovered.

## 10 ANY LADY, GENTLEMEN OR OTHER WHO HAS ATTAINED MAJORITY MAY CHOOSE TO BECOME A WARAL.

Ailtaxots history of Wilders translated and distributed by the first Silver scribe of Lundinium. Partial manuscript stored in an undisclosed location in Maji, Central America. (Accounts composed in 958 AD)

Chelone the serpentine city of the tortoise...

The great civilisation of Chelone was not always spread across the world. It started as a small collection of villages arranged in a semi-circle. When the village grew it had to expand across the terrain and across the seas, but it always retained a penchant for constructing series of villages arranged as a succession of semi-circles. The Warals like to think of Chelone as a serpentine civilisation. Indeed, when the ancient Waral Wilders managed to dance above the skies they reported that, viewed from the clouds, the tortoise civilisation of Chelone looked more like a snake slithering its way across the globe. The Waral Wilders expanded their methods, and soon they were able to dance above the dominions of the Dragoons as well. When Chelonian and Dragoon runaways decided to unite with the Warals, they were accepted with open arms. The former prisoners were surprised to discover that any lady, gentlemen or other who has attained majority may choose to become a Waral. The runaways we agreeably surprised to find out that following the Waral way of life is a choice, and a wise choice it was.

## 11 THE WARAL WAY OF LIFE STANDS BETWEEN THE CONSTRAINTS OF CHELONE AND THE STRICT RULE OF THE DRAGOONS.

Ancient philosophical thoughts of Xjame engraved on a single cylinder. Translated and distributed by the Scribe of the fog. Artefacts on display at the history museum in Cairo, North Africa. (Cylinder dating from 3000BC, translated manuscript composed in late 1499 AD.)

Chances of Xjame…

Xjame was a passionate historian. She came to the conclusion that history had never been shaped by great leaders, history was shaped by great events accomplished by all of us. The extinction of the sacred giants, the disappearance of the elementals and the primordials, the reclusion of the Waral Wilders… All was connected. Xjame found answers when exploring the possibility of the existence of freak of natures. The search for the perfect being was not fruitful. Indeed the freak of nature is tall, beautiful, never sick. The freak of nature is intelligent, formidable, fantastic, perfect and frankly… doesn't exist. Xjame soon found out that the largest and the healthiest have the same chances. Xjame soon deduced that the old and the sick do not necessarily die first! It appeared that perfection did not exist. Perfection couldn't exist. The essence of life and death remained in the power of will, dedication, love and ethical thinking. The mind and the body were perhaps not separate phenomenons, no. Body and mind were in fact part of the same exact occurrence: human history. The conclusion was the following: normality was only a myth. Xiame was fortunate, as this Waral was able flourish standing between the constraints of Chelone and strict rule of the Dragoons.

## 12 THE WARALS RECOGNISE THAT HUMANITY SERVES NATURE, NOT THE OTHER WAY AROUND.

Tirade from the Big Wars tablets, dating from around 4000 BC. Relic discovered and translated by the second Purple scribe in 1641 AD. (Manuscript first distributed in 1644 AD.)

A Wilders motivation…

Long after the battle against the armies of stones, long after the giant wars, long after the end of the elementals and the primordials exploits. Long after the conflicts between the elephant riders and the bull riders, long after the poisoned wars and the envenomed tactics of suppression there was a Waral Wilder walking across the long-forgotten battle fields looking for artefacts. This wilder had visited countless burials mounds all over the globe, reciting summons along the way. This wilder was an instructor, one of many guardians of the ancient Waral ways. This wilder had two peculiar words of wisdom. The first was, according to an ancient war story, that this Wilder had tried to wet her toes in the river of deception. The waters of trickery revealed to be much too cold for her taste. Her conclusion was that strong minds are usually discussed by the rivers of profiteering and usurpation. This was in reference to an event in which the Wilder was approached by a battalion of Dragoons during one of her many searches across the land. The Dragoons wanted to bribe the Waral in order to bend the history of certain artefacts that, if discovered, would have put the rule of the Dragoons under scrutiny. The battalion bullied the Waral Wilder, but in vain. The strong mind of the followers of the Waral way of life are not for sale. The Dragoons wanted the Waral to tamed nature, as their regal doctrine insured them that nature was at the service of humanity. The Wilder refused and said : "The Warals recognise that humanity serves nature, not the other way around. This is why we call is the laws of nature, not the laws of men." The Dragoons laughed and left after administering a correction. Shortly after this altercation with the Dragoons battalion, this Wilder was approached by the Council of Chelone. The council asked the Wilder to simply ignore some of her recently discovered artefacts. The council was determined to burry certain dark chapters involving the civilisation of Chelone during the big wars. Artefacts and burial mounds revealed a worldwide connection. A connection that was for a long time dismissed. This Waral was determined to expose the truth, notably that both the Dragoon rulers and the Council of Chelone shared the same responsibility and the same fears. The motivation of this valiant Wilder deterred her from caving in to the demands made by the Council of Chelone. It appeared that dishonesty, ignorance and laziness required too much villainy and maleficent organisation in order to cultivate ignore and dismissal. All the pictographs, inscriptions and funeral rituals pointed to a long forgotten common culture. All the blocks, cylinders, songs and scrolls shared a common origin. This Wilder was determined to unravel the truth. This Waral instructor was one of the first to initiate the creation of Waral sanctuaries. These Waral sanctuaries would, in time provide safe grounds for all the followers of the Waral way of life and for all the curious minds. These safe grounds, focused on history, education, medicine and agriculture, would not start to appear after the death of this valiant Wilder. A popular Waral tale states that this Wilder instructor's name was never disclosed. Her direct descendants had no knowledge of her title of instructor, nor did they know that she was in fact the first recognised Wilder until the end of the tenth century. When asked about the incredible exploits of their matriarch, the descendants of this valiant Waral Wilder, simply refer to her as the first Purple scribe and keeper of truth.

## 13 THE WARALS TRAVEL WITH THE ESSENTIAL BLOOM WHEREVER THEY GO.

Remaining chapter of the Botanix, also known as the book of medicines and poisons. Original scroll dating from the second century AD. Discovered by Dene Benali and translated by the first Green scribe. Scroll on display at the Smithsonian museum, North America. (Discovered and translated in 1859 AD)

The origin of the Botanix and the essential bloom:

Hermerut was the personal healer of the ruler of the northern provinces of A'Ferika. Hermerut had no desire to serve under a Dragoon ruler, but didn't have a choice. Hermerut was the most talented healer in the land and was kept prisoner in the ruler's palace. Hermerut's knowledge was so great that the captive Waral was forced to develop and expand the gardens of the Dragoon ruler. The gardens were separated into four distinct patches; one for the eatable fruits, vegetables and spices, one for the aromatic plants in order to compliment meals, perfume the Dragoons regal court and to expose a collection of exotic specimens. The third patch was mostly dedicated to textile plants, herbs and grasses. The fourth patch was kept under the strict control of the Dragoon's personal guard. This patch contained medicinal and poisonous plants. When the Dragoon ruler decided that Hermermut's services were no longer needed, the healer was banished from the continent. Hermermut was to resume a Waral life, but was not able to return home. So Hermermut as well as a group of wondering followers of the Waral way of life built the first sanctuary. The first step was to start a garden in order to feed, clothe, heal and maintain the sanctuary. All the Warals worked hard; they prepared four gardens, all of them square shaped. The four squared patches were united as one large square divided in four equal parts. When Hermermut was asked to plant the first seed in the garden, the former captive did so. Hermermut planted the first essential bloom's seed. The seed was planted in the exact centre of the large garden. Hermermut justified this act by claiming: "This essential bloom's seed will grow into an essential plant. Once full grown the plant will touch all four gardens. For its stems produce the strongest textile. It's roots and leaves will provide much needed nourishment. Its fruits are able to heal the deepest wounds and its flowers will enhance the smell of your bouquets". Indeed, as mint, sage, rosemary, lavender, ginger, paper birch, frilled oaks and chrysanthemum grew on one part of the garden, cabbage, kale, carrots, roots, grains, berries, beans, tomatoes, corn, apples, cactus and dandelions grew on an other. The third patch was reserved for hibiscus, passion flowers, ligustrum, lentos, papyrus, myosotis, marry golds and other delightful specimens. The last part of the garden contained different types of sage, mints, absinth, berries, thyme, laurels, aquatic plants and other specimens of medicinal properties. And in the centre of the garden grew the essential bloom. The essential bloom was the name given to different types of hemp, some coming from across the world. Every hemp variety had its own specialty, but each could be used to manufacture textile, feed the residents of the sanctuary, heal the external as well as internal wounds and was used as a necessary element of perfumes and aesthetics. Since then, this plant is known by the Warals as the essential bloom and they travel with it wherever they go.

# II Growth and nutrition:

The Parisian authorities had already set up a perimeter around the Louis XVI Park, a small neighbourhood park. Police wagons were stationed at the intersection of the Haussmann Boulevard and a tiny street called rue Pasquier. The authorities strongly believed that this was the site where the target had originally been released into the air. As we suited up, we quickly noticed that the surrounding population was acting in a very bizarre manner. Some individuals were having a laugh, others looked as if they were possessed while some just appeared to be in some sort of frenetic trance. There was a visible look of terror on the faces of some of these individuals. None of the civilians paid any attention to our team, who wore face masks and were dressed in brightly coloured protective gear. Curiously, not a soul seemed to register the presence of our massive drone. The Delivery Station, the new and expensive flying piece of equipment, had landed on the parkway near the park just moments earlier. It appeared as if the infected individuals were under a spell. There was also a small group of weirdoes who were dressed up as monks with huge hoods covering their faces. They were just standing there among the rest of the panicked Parisians. When we found the source of this unbelievable scene, our agency as well as the Parisian authorities were shocked. The madness and chaos were caused by the pollen of a remarkable species of flowering plant. The plant had obviously been recently planted in and around the park. These beautiful but fatal plants were spreading a toxic compound present in their pollen. This pollen drove any person breathing it towards a path of either euphoria or total fright. This air born hallucinogen was dividing the city into a mix of absolute panic and a complete zombiesque vegetative state. The Police forced and our team had to act quickly. The perimeter had to be secured and any infected and non-affected civilians evacuated from the zone. We took all the necessary precautions; we jarred and bagged enough specimens and samples of residues for later analysis. We were then forced to dispose of all remaining plants on site. The next intervention took place in the grounds of Les Invalides. The local population was going berserk, some individuals were getting intoxicated more rapidly than others. The effects produced by the pollen emanating from the toxic plant affected individuals differently.

It took about forty-eight hours for the effects of the pollen to dissipate. It took us less than that to realise what we were dealing with. As we examined all the samples and specimens back in the Delivery Station, Babs analysis revealed some remarkably interesting findings. First, this plant was not part of the flowers ordered by the city. Therefore, it had to have been dumped or planted deliberately. The second interesting finding was that the large bright flowers appeared to belong to the genus Datura, a large and toxic tropical plant with flowers resembling drooping trumpets. But the pollen and root systems of this plant looked completely unnatural. The flowers looked like Datura trumpets, the aroma of the leaves resembled that of cannabis and the roots of this mysterious plant looked like the roots of a plant called Acanthus. This was definitely a manmade organism; this was a robust hybrid created with a purpose. Thirdly, we concluded that this spectacular bio threat incident would certainly repeat itself. But a few questions persisted; who was the creator of this plant? When was this plant created? And why? All these queries remained a mystery to us, at least for the moment.

Not even a week after our intervention in Paris, the Anti-Bioterrorism and Bio-threat Agency was contacted by the department of environmental relations of Port au Prince in Ayïti. As we all expected, a similar incident was unraveling. The mysterious plant had already started to spread in the Caribbean Islands. The Delivery Station had to be operational and ready to fly. The colossal drone landed in Port au Prince a few hours after receiving the call for help. Zed was always amazed by the speed and stealth of our flying laboratory. The young woman had been living in the drone since the beginning of its construction. She had brought her pet Jackson's chameleon as well as her personal lab equipment on board. Zed was very satisfied with the stability of the drone during a flight. However, Les was not surprised, nor impressed by the rapidity and precision of the Delivery Station for the simple reason that he had previously flown much faster and much dangerous crafts. The proper functionality and safety of the team, as well as the outside of the drone, is Les Roken's responsibility. We, the nerds, are responsible for the research, the tests and the results. We are basically in charge of everything that is going inside the Delivery Station's laboratory.

The situation in Ayïti was far from being under control when we arrived. This time Les had to deploy our security team to set up a safety perimeter around the infected zone. The job was completed promptly. Margaret got her samples and Mehdi was able to reassure the civilians and calm down the situation with the local officials. Noël got the opportunity to compare the specimens collected in Port au Prince with the samples collected in New Gaul a few days earlier. You probably remember that the palace that was destroyed last century by an earthquake has been rebuilt. It is now the most splendid piece of modern architecture in the Caribbean. The new palace is viewed as a symbol of overcoming feats. Right after our intervention in Port au Prince, the A.B.B.A. team was quietly packing the equipment and getting ready to head back to our headquarters in Washington D.C. when Noël ran towards me bearing a wild look in his eyes and screamed:

"Zed, Sam, Babs, Mehd, Les, guys! Florida! Florida! Oh, putin de bordel de merde! For fuck snakes! Sam, we need to fly the drone to Florida immediatement!"

"What now, chap?" I asked a bit confused.

"The Governor of Florida" Noël continued" Governor… erm… Governor Whoever the Fuck, just called. He says that he needs us in Boca Baton like, yesterday!"

And so, began our swift and critical series of interventions across the world. The protocol was simple and effective. First, to create a secured perimeter around the infected zone. Second, proceed to collect enough samples and specimens for later studies. Third, to eradicate the organic and invasive threat. And finally, pack the equipment as fast as possible and fly the Station in the direction of the next infected area. (Whew!)

Noël, the entire team and I used the entire drone both as the most up-To-date laboratory and as a flying hotel. The Delivery Station was overcrowded, but not without positive results. Zed and I got plenty of time to explore the secrets of this plant. It multiplied via an extremely rapid root growth, producing long runners looking to conquer a larger territory. If a single root fragment remains on site, it will develop into an entire new and mature flowering plant in a matter of days. If unattended each root fragment, or runner, can give birth to a whole flowering patch in less than a week. The largest flowers mature within hours and always liberate small pouches of pollen during the sunniest part of the day. When the pouches of pollen become air born and drift away from their mother plants, they start to release a toxic compound with troubling qualities. When humans breathe this compound present in the pollen, they soon fall victim of miscarriage, fertility loss and a strong burst of hallucinations that can last up to three days. This pollen was acting as an air born birth control. In addition, and just as troubling, as mentioned earlier, the hallucinations provoked by the toxic plant can affect the subjects in one of two ways. Some individuals are subjected to violent panic attacks accompanied by paranoia and exaggerated fears and some individuals become, on the contrary, numb, relaxed and appear to be in a soporific trance. Babs was very helpful in many ways, not only did she managed to isolate and replicate the compound, but she also developed a preventive treatment. The treatment had to be administered before the subject was exposed to the pollen to counter the infertility as well as the hallucinatory effects. If administered after exposure to the pollen, the treatment can suppress the hallucinations in an instant, but unfortunately it cannot restore fertility. One day, when we completed an operation in Chennai, one of our colleagues, a local Commissioner, gave us a call and invited my old friend and myself to the nearest police station. This police Commissioner and former professor at the Madras Agricultural Centre, informed me that the author of these recent bio-terrorist acts had given himself up to him. Noël and I were asked to interrogate the bio-terrorist in question. My old friend turned white as a ghost when he heard the name of this individual known to the South Asian authorities by the name of Stanley T. Yashwanti. Noël informed me that

Yashwanti was one of the main symbols for the Warals. The Warals, whom I perceived at the time as an ancient and cryptic group of nature worshippers. Indeed, my old friend rarely talked about his fascination for the Waral way of life. But on that day, everything changed and consequently the focus became clearer to me than ever before. Noël and I stepped into the holding cell. A good looking young man, sporting a neatly trimmed handlebar moustache laid eyes upon my old friend and proclaimed:

"I am Yashwanti, the Bengal monitor, the witness. I am the mighty Dragoon Waral from Chelone. Ferika sent me. I traveled to Chennai from the old city in search of the next leader of the ancient Dragoons dynasty of Chelone."

Noël took me by the shoulder and whispered in my ear:

"A Dragoon Waral from Chelone named Yashwanti? This is going to be interesting".

"Why is that, mate?" I asked.

"You see Sam," Noël continued, "a Waral cannot be a Dragoon no more than a Dragoon can claim to be a Waral. And I'll tell you something else, mon ami, I know this guy and he ain't from around here."

Noël turned to Yashwanti and said:

"Okay, Stanley, game's over, loose the shitty fake beard and the phoney accent."

"All right. You got me, now what?" asked Yashwanti while stripping off his fake whiskers. "And who the fuck do you think you are all of a sudden'?"

"You know perfectly well who I am. I am Noël Joseph Douglass Buenaparte Israël the Third and Marquis de Degeulis. Now tell us everything you know!," instructed my old friend. Noël, being an orphan, loved to use a series of fictitious and borrowed names, including mine, every time a person would ask for his full name.

"Well, the Dragoons have been busy, they asked me to spread the word and saw the seeds of reckoning. I have traveled far and wide with the roots of The Cleanser." Yashwanti looked at the ceiling of the holding cell and started to rock himself back and forth, while repeating the name Ferika over and over. I quietly sang in the direction of my old friend:

"Who is this cheeky wanker? Doo... doo... doo..."

Noël answered me in the same manner without missing a beat:

"He is a former anthropology student of mine, ska ba doo bap... from Brighton University, long story, ska ba da boo..."

My old friend began to bombard Stanley with a succession of precise and technical inquiries about the invasive plant and the person known as Ferika. The answers provided by the disturbed man were vague, to say the least, and gravely incorrect. I distinctly remember Noël asking:

"How did you manage to find stable PH in the soil before planting these demonic flowers?"

"Oh well, it was pretty easy" confessed Stanley with a very cocky tone in his voice, "my flowers can conquer any PH, you twat!"

In fact, this invasive plant was able to develop in only certain types of soil, containing extremely strict PH level between 7.1 and 8.3. Noël's former student had lost his wits; Stanley had no idea what PH in the soil even meant. My old friend and I eventually left the detainment facility; there was no point in arguing with Stanley. Our team was running out of time; we had to halt this interview. The disturbed man was to be kept under strict medical observation. It didn't take long for Noël and the local authorities to deduce that the man was just a looney and a mere imposter. It was fairly easy to figure out that this sick man had only provided historically and scientifically crooked answers. For example, our lab tests led the A. B. B. A. team to the conclusion that the plant we were desperately trying to eradicate had a peculiar love for soils poor in organic matter and a severe penchant for clay, rocky grounds, surrounded by mortar and concrete. In essence, this invasive species was only targeting cities.

A prolonged investigation revealed that Stanley Yashwanti had previously been involved in public demonstrations and violent protests, denouncing the malefic intents behind the Mechanic Revolutionaries' activities in orbit. The end game of the Mechanics is to liberate the Earthican population from itself by colonising other worlds. After terrorising and infiltrating every space station, including the International Earthican Station, some Mechanics renegades claimed all Non-Terran property as their own. They built their headquarters on the moon and they already have colonised it. The rumour is that they already have more than one base on Mars. In other words, the Mechanics now own everything and everyone leaving the Earth's orbit. Stanley Yashwanti, like many other conspiracy theorists, has been using extremely brutal ideologies to spread chaos. He directly borrowed ideas from the Natural Liberation Front's doctrine, while exploiting misleading and misinterpreted stories about the Waral's way of life. This was to scare the shite out of uninformed and naive citizens all around him. The reality is that a polarised group of public opinions has recently emerged. A real animosity between the Mechanics sympathisers and the Natural Front supporters started to flood most capitals and sister cites around the globe. Only Reykjavik hasn't been affected yet for some reason. Yashwanti had been put under observation since his arrival in the Indian region, but he gave himself up right after the mysterious flowering plant suddenly appeared in Chennai. During questioning, Stan Yashwanti had tried to tell us briefly about a man named Saint Bernard or Bernard or something like that, but he soon praised the mysterious Ferika.

After this extraordinary interlude, Noël had more questions than I did. My old friend was particularly curious about why the man had chosen the surname Yashwanti, as this was not Stanley's real name. Was the name Yashwanti a random name chosen to provoke the followers of the Waral way of life? Was it a simple homage to the famous monitor lizard who bears the same name? And most importantly: did Stanley know the full story of Yashwanti and its significance for the Warals? My objective was to complete my assignment; to eradicate this toxic and invasive plant. I soon realised that Noël was becoming more obsessed with the Waral's history.

After a much-anticipated governmental call from Washington D. C., in North America, General Lesley Roken became suddenly excited and apprehensive. The idea of re-uniting with some of his old military and politician friend made him somehow a tad nervous. What pushed me to hire Les in the first place was his exemplary military record. These days, Les and I share more than a professional relationship. We share a career and a life. I met Les many years ago when the Agency was looking to hire a new security chief. One night, I met an incredibly bright and handsome man at a men's club in Northern Virginia. After a simple greeting, I realised that I was speaking to the man that I was to interview the next day. I recognised his picture from the CV I had received from him a few weeks earlier. We talked all night, and I interviewed him for the job the next morning. We have been inseparable ever since. Years later we are still together and looking forward to start a family of our own.

## 14 ANY WARAL HAS THE AUTHORITY TO BUILD A NEW SANCTUARY.

Chapter six from the book entitled "Legality and Warality" dating from the late 17th century AD. Translated by the second Red scribe in 1867 AD Manuscript privately owned by M.T.R. (Copied and distributed in December 1868 AD)

### I Sanctuary definition and organisation:

i. A Waral Sanctuary is a sacred and peaceful location, revolving around education and reflection by the followers of the Waral way of life. Any Waral has the authority to build a new Sanctuary. Any potential, current, or future follower of the Waral way of life entering a Sanctuary is considered a Walker.

ii. Any citizen of the Earth is welcomed in a Waral Sanctuary. A Sanctuary is directed by a Council, or board, composed of followers of the Waral way of life who have completed a vision and at least one walkabout.

iii. In the case of a newly formed Sanctuary created by a single follower of the Waral way of life, this Waral shall be acting both as the Monitor and the Council. Newly formed Sanctuaries under the direction of a single individual are known as mono-Sanctuaries, until new Walkers choose to join and be a part of the Council.

iv. The Council, or board, is composed of instructors, or officers. An instructor, or officer, needs to have a deep knowledge of the history of the Waral way of life as well as a deep understanding of local and global cultural laws. An instructor, or officer, must have completed a vision, at least one walkabout and possess the desire to start a phase of construction through the creation of a Sanctuary. The phase of construction can be achieved dependably or independently of a Waral Sanctuary, although going through a phase of construction, or participation, is much more comfortable and effective when realised within the frame of a Sanctuary.

v. Instructors, or officers, are regarded as main teachers.

Any Waral on the Council, or board, is considered an Instructor. The Monitor, or chair, or main Instructor, presides over the Sanctuary's Council. The Monitor, or chair, is responsible for the Sanctuary's thriving, peaceful and healthy organisation.

a. The Monitor, or chair, speaks for the Sanctuary. The Monitor is the highest executive authority of the Sanctuary, followed by the Mediator, the Orator, the Scribe, the Accountant and finally, the Walkers present in, or around the Sanctuary at the time.
b. The Mediator, or vice chair, is responsible of the Sanctuary during the Monitor's absence. The Mediator speaks for the Sanctuary during the Monitors absence. The Mediator shall succeed or replace the Monitor during exceptional occasions.
c. The Orator, or delegate, shall replace the Monitor and the Mediator if both are exceptional absent. The Orator, or delegate, shall speak for the Sanctuary on special occasions.
d. The Scribe, or secretary, shall keep written, typed or engraved records and documenting the duration of the sessions, meetings and committees. The Scribe, or secretary, is in charge of sending out announcements, keeping track of the agenda and assuring that the organisation's records are maintained.

e. The Accountant, or treasurer, is responsible for the finances of the Sanctuary and shall make a report at each Council, or board, session, meeting or committee.

vi. The security and the continuation of the Waral ethical code of conduct will be supported and enforced by each individual. Querulous arguments and events must be resolved in a peaceful and orderly fashion. If querulous or security concerns cannot be peacefully agreed upon, the Monitor shall take lawful and exemplary actions in order to stop said querulous events.

vii. New legislations or revisions can be submitted to the Council by any resident of the Sanctuary. These legislative propositions can only be approved and voted by the Council, or board.

viii. Supernatural elevation nor divine adoration, although dearly respected, is encouraged in a Sanctuary. A Sanctuary revolves around education, history, science, biology, the arts and many more subjects developed by ordinary individuals. A sanctuary may be inclined to update its knowledge of local tax laws and other legislatures in order to coexist with the land where the Sanctuary is located.

ix. Individual beliefs and practices as well as the search for wisdom are encouraged in a Waral Sanctuary. Sacred practices as well as the scientific worship of nature are encouraged in a Waral Sanctuary.

x. The activities conducted in a Waral Sanctuary include, but not limited to: reflection, historical and scientific education, artistic development, volunteering, gardening, cooking, cleaning, tutoring, learning, sharing, discovering the path to Warality, neighbourly love, respect, acceptance, vitality, diversity, responsibility and more.

## 2 Waral Sanctuary details of operation:

A. Name and purpose:

Name examples: Waral Sanctuary of..., Waral Cultural Centre of..., Cultural Waral Sanctuary of...

B. Mission:

The purpose of a Waral Sanctuary organisation is exclusively for charitable, educational and scientific purposes. Especially to preserve, protect and share the Waral cultural heritage as well as to provide a structure and land oriented towards reflection, education and learning.

C. Membership:

Membership shall essentially consist of the members of the Council, or board of directors, as well as followers of the Waral way of life, desiring to reside in the Sanctuary. Walkers, visitors and other followers of the Waral way of life who do not reside in the Sanctuary are always welcomed and considered temporarily members.

## 3 Meetings:

The date, time and place of the annual meeting shall be set by the Council, or board.

Special meetings may be called by the Monitor, or chair, as well by the instructors, or executive committee.

Notice of each meeting shall be given to each voting member by letter, dispatch, carrier pigeon or any mode of communication available, not less than seven full days before the meetings.

## 4 The Council, or board of directors:

The Council shall have up to 10 members. The Council receives no compensation other than reasonable expenses.

1) The Council shall meet at least once every season, or every three months, at an agreed upon time and place in order to review past, present and future events.

2) Election of new Council members (or re-election and or validation of existing council members in some cases) will occur as the first item of business at the annual meeting of the Sanctuary, or organisation.
3) All Council members shall serve eight seasons, or two years, but are eligible for re-election.
4) A quorum, a query, a requests or a meeting must be attended by at least fifty-one percent of the Council members before business can be transacted, motioned, or passed.
5) An official meeting requires that each Council member has written, typed or sung about agreeing to the meeting at least seven days in advance.
6) There shall be five officers of the Council, or board, consisting of; a Monitor, or chair, a Mediator, or vice chair, a Scribe, or secretary, an Accountant, or treasurer, and an Orator, or relation delegate. A Waral residing in a mono-Sanctuary must assume all roles until the mono-Sanctuary is joined by others.
7) The Council member duties are as follow:
i. The Monitor, or chair, presides over the Sanctuary's Council. The Monitor, or chair, is responsible for the Sanctuary's thriving, peaceful and healthy organisation.
ii. The Mediator, Vice chair, is responsible for the Sanctuary during the Monitor's absence.
iii. The Orator, or delegate, shall replace the Monitor and the Mediator if both are absent. The Orator, or delegate, shall speak for the Sanctuary on special occasions.
iv. The Scribe, or secretary, shall keep written, typed or engraved records and timing of the sessions, meetings and committees. The Scribe, or secretary, is in charge of sending out announcements, keeping

track of the agenda and assuring the organisation's records are maintained.

v. The Accountant, or treasurer, is responsible for the supervision and the management of the finances of the Sanctuary and shall make a report at each Council, or board, session, meeting and committee.

vi. In the case of a mono-Sanctuary, the mono-Monitor shall assume all duties noted above until the Sanctuary is joined by other followers of the Waral way of life.

8) When a vacancy on the Council exists, nominations of a new member may be from present Council members by the Scribe two weeks in advance of the Council meeting, unless noted otherwise.

9) Resignation from the Council must be in writing, inscribed or pressed and received by the Scribe. A Council member shall be dropped from the Council due to excessive absences. 'Excessive' is defined as more than three unexcused absences from the Council in a calendar year. A Council member may also be removed for other reasons by a three-fourths vote of the remaining members of the Council.

10) Special meetings of the Council shall be called upon the request of the Monitor or one-third of the Council members. Notices of special meetings shall be sent by the scribe to each member two weeks in advance, unless noted otherwise.

### 5 Committees:

The Council may create committees, as needed, such as discussions, fundraising, projects, archives, presentations, volunteering... The Monitor appoints all committee members. The Council serves as the executive committee council.

The Monitor must preside over and supervise committees.

The Accountant is chair of the finance committee, including which includes three additional Council members. The finance committee is responsible for developing and reviewing fiscal, financial, budgetary and volunteering plans with the Council members and other members. The Council must approve the budget. In addition, all expenditures must be approved by the Council or executive committee. The fiscal year shall be the calendar year, accompanying the seasons. Annual reports shall be submitted to the Council, outlining income, expenditures, pending income and volunteering. Records must be made available for all. The Scribe as well as the Accountant may be asked for assistance in order to formulate and archive said records.

### 6 Amendments:

Bylaws may be amended, when necessary, by a two-thirds majority vote of the Council. Proposed amendments, new propositions or modifications must be submitted to the Monitor or the Scribe to be sent out with regular meeting announcements, unless noted other wise.

Sanctions and modifications must be approved and determined by a two-thirds majority vote of the council.

New lands and new areas that are desired have the potential of becoming a Sanctuary. The desire to create a Sanctuary need not necessarily be communicated by the local authorities where the future Sanctuary is to be located but is strongly encouraged both as a legislative act and a gesture of respect to the added community.

## 15 NO WARAL IS BORN A WARAL. TO ATTAIN WARALITY IS A CHOICE; IT IS NEITHER HEREDITARY NOR CAN IT BE IMPOSED ON ANYONE.

Passage from the Waral chart, composed in the early 18th century AD by Juoenür. Translated by the second Silver Scribe. Document in storage at the Grand library of Reykjavik, Icelandic Isles. (Translation first distributed in early 1928 AD)

Warality inside and outside of a Sanctuary:

To seek a state of Warality, a state of peace and purpose, is a choice. No Waral is born a Waral; following the Waral way of life is a choice and is not hereditary. Therefore, this path cannot be forced or imposed on any other citizen of the Earth, dead or alive. Many phrases and words can help map the way towards a state of Warality. In order to assist old and new followers of the Waral way of life to attain a state of Warality, a list of thoughts has been gathered and collected over the ages. This list, is an ever-growing list:

Thank you, thank you for everything.

Beaten, often. Defeated, never.

Life, longevity, prosperity.

All is good, all is fine.

In unity there is strength; no one is truly alone.

To lift the veil of confusion is to free the mind.

Dogs have owners; but cats are the owners. Humans are free.

Those who no longer complain are familiar with the road of pain. Warality will bring a peaceful map.

If you need to ask something to the Monitor, you'd better do it quickly.

The more you know, the more it hurts, but Warality and wisdom are essential elements toward the path of healing.

Sometimes ignorance is bliss, but never be afraid of open the minds of others.

It appears that everything is a joke, or nothing is.

The sick one is not necessarily the one who is next to die. Take time to heal.

Most dream about big plans, big expenses and fat finances. It is so much easier to take it step by step. Envision a small achievement at a time and outgrow it.

It must be noted that cultures travel faster than populations.

Humans share information, ideas and techniques almost as often as it rains.

Many pick the fruits, but few study the roots. To study the entire plant is an integral part of Warality.

Patience is the greatest of allies.

One who walks across the land and dances between cultures has excellent Waral potential.

A Waral seeks peace and Warality, independent of deities or regality.

A follower of the Waral way of life must honour the path towards Warality.

Warality is a state of peace, connection, reflection, peacefulness and compassion.

## 16 WARALITY IS A WARAL'S PEACE OF MIND AS WELL AS A WARAL'S PIECE OF MIND.

Passage from "The Instructor's manual", ancient manuscript dating from around 300 BC. Translated and distributed by the second Anonymous scribe. Relic on display at the Ancient History Museum of the Northern territories, North America. (First copy distributed in June 1985 AD)

## The path towards Warality: vision, walkabout and construction.

Every individual, as the name implies, possesses an individual view on the world. Every individual has an individual personality, individual desires, individual identity and individual beliefs. The connection between these attributes, as well as the realisation that introgression regarded as an organic process and a methodology are facets of the same occurrence , notably existence. This existence results in what is called a vision of the world with a goal and an objective.

## The speculation, preparation and embodiment of a Waral's view of the world is called a vision.

Every situation has its own sets of rules and principles. Each of these situations have the potential to lead to exceptions. A particular set of circumstances that renders a rule of a principle inapplicable. Therefore, it is safe to assume that, in a way, every individual has the potential to navigate between natural as well as mechanical rules and principles. This navigation is characterised by a certain desire and possibility of achieving a walkabout. A walk about is a personal journey in which a Waral will travel in order to develop her or his vision.

Every individual who has achieved the realisation of a vision as well as the completion of a walkabout may be compelled to go through a process of construction. The construction is a phase in which a follower of the Waral way of life decides to contribute to joyful responsibility of being a Waral. Notably the pursuit of education, knowledge, wisdom, Warality, participation and or creation of a Sanctuary and much more.

The vision, the walkabout and the construction process are integral parts of the lives of those who follow the Waral way of life. Every step is a step towards a piece of mind, a peace of mind and a mental state affectionally coined as Warality. In order to attain the state of Warality, one must allow herself, or himself to possess a flexible and exceptional vision of the world. Warality can be attained from any Sanctuary, land or any place.

Once a vision occurs, one may want to explore different methods, different visions and different surroundings by starting a mental and physical walkabout. This can be achieved by simply walking or traveling. Some Warals may not be able to move very far, while others may be able to move further. Some Warals may not be fortunate enough to be mobile. These Warals must share their small movements with even more optimism. Travels, no matter how short or long, forge the character and will even open the most closed minds. When a Waral has the desire to start the process of construction, this Waral must be prepared. The construction is a step-by-step process resulting in a state of Warality. It must be cherished. A Waral's reality is a Waral's most precious asset. This reality follows a Waral's peace of mind as Warality's piece of mind is omnipresent, ready to learn, determined to discover new places, hungry for knowledge as well as the study of different cultures. Most of all, the Warality is rooted in unity. For Warality is an act of unity, levity, serenity and determination.

The state of Warality will forge the perception of an individual's reality for every single person. The core of the Waral way of life rests upon the shoulders of those who, voluntarily or not, dance between different cultures and connections of knowledge. This mental process is the essence of a Waral's humanity, diversity and responsibility, as defined by the Waral way of life.

The three important steps in the life of a Waral, notably the vision, one or more walkabouts as well as the desire to ignite a phase of construction will undeniably lead to a pronounced fondness for certain methods, protocols or rituals. These methods are of great help to assist a follower of the Waral way of life to enter a serene state of mind known as reflection.

Any hatchling, walker or visitor should be encouraged to reflect on one's life, action, abilities and desires. This reflective state of mind is known by the Warals as Summons. Summons do not lie, nor they revolve around supernatural hopes and beliefs. Summons cannot be compared to prayers nor demands. Summons are personal contracts between a Waral and the series of events which the follower of the Waral way of life is reflecting upon. A Summon is a mental and physical motivation or validation of one's actions. A Summon will not affect the health, funds, happiness or any source of the reflection. A Summon will affect the follower of the Waral way of life's decisions regarding said reflection.

### Summons guidelines:

Some followers of the Waral way of life may choose to make use of artefact, articles and totems to help said Waral to enter a state of reflection in order to summon. These articles include, but are not limited to: candles, ensigns, aromas, drinkable liquids, tobacco, essential bloom, sage and other herbs.

Anything that will help a follower of the Waral way of life achieve a reflective state and therefore help said Waral to realise her or his goal.

Personal or sharable, every summon, celebration or Memorium is regarded as a Summon type of ceremony. As mentioned above, a Summon doesn't rest upon the shoulders of hope or prayers, no. A Summon is a realistic and ethical moral contract; a moral contract between the follower of the Waral way of life and the source of the reflection of said Waral. Some Warals are persuaded that any type of summon is represented by a Waral's ability to acknowledge her or his link with the elemental world. In other words, some followers of the Waral way of life may feel a deep connection with the natural world that they perceive themselves and nature as one single entity. They become, in a sense, nothing more than a simple organism representing an essential cog in the incredible mechanics of existence. A Summon is an achievable contract that is achieved and sealed when it is realised. A Waral is entirely responsible for the successful results of a Summon.

Reflective Summons, celebrations and Memoria are always conducted with the utmost honesty and dedication. None of these Summonses will bear any results if not conducted with positivity, appreciation, and as state before, a total honesty towards the source of the reflective summon, celebration or Memorium. These activities can be conducted at any time and any place. In fact, the presence or absence of a Sanctuary will not affect said activities. Any summon, celebration or Memorium can be conducted at home, outdoors, indoors, in an urban or provincial environment. A Sanctuary will provide a safe, quiet and dedicated environment for any type of summon, celebration or Memorium. Each activity can be conducted by a single Waral or more. Each activity is conducted according to the desire of the participant or participants.

### The reflective summon:

The reflective summon is a personal state of reflection, or meditation. It can be performed alone or in groups. The reflective summon can be oriented towards a certain goal or desire that must be realistic and achievable. This reflective state is not based on hope or faith, the reflective summon is a motivational demand imposed on one self. Many or no totems, candles, ensigns, herbs

or perhaps after said Memorium. The Memorium can be performed by one or many Warals, the ceremony is usually accompanied by culinary exchanges, plants and other flowering gifts, speeches, a series of summons, possible entertainment etc...

One must focus on the source of the Memorium, silence or music on the contrary may help attendees to focus, grieve, and reveal natural distress. To honour the source of the memories, one must be able to let go, peacefully.

Any reflective Summon, Celebration or Memorium is, to the followers of the Waral way of life, a way to express an intimate connection with personal introgression, both as an organic principle and a methodology. Indeed introgression as an organic principle is the process of inheritance of genetic (organic) elements across generations. In turn introgression, as a methodology, is regarded as the inheritance of ideological and technical (methodologies) elements across generations.

## 17 THE MOST IMPORTANT LAW OF THE WARAL WAY OF LIFE IS: ONE LAW, ONE LOVE.

Article from the Global Theological revue entitled "Preliminary study of the meaning and implications of introgression for the followers of the Waral way of life" redacted by the Shiny scribe. (Published on October 6th 2028 AD)

Introgression is defined as an organic, then as a moral process. Include definition of admixture and define the difference between introgression as a moral process opposed to simple introspection.

Introgression, both as an organic process and a methodology, have an impact on what is perceived as the natural and mechanical world. The Waral way of life regards both aspects integral parts of existence.

In the beginning, the first followers of the Waral way of life developed their own calendar. This calendar represented by the denouement of the seasons was often accompanied by festivities, independent of any type of summon. These festivities, commonly called seasonal festivities, are the reflection of the passage of time seen through the eyes of the seasons and their development. Some festivities are underlined by stories and myths while others revolve around certain events that, as the whole participate in the continuation of the Waral way of life. As the followers of the Waral way of life regard the meaning of life, or existence, as the succession of survival, adaptation and evolution, the Waral also recognise that the purpose of mankind, or the meaning of mankind, is that our humanity allows us to travel against the wind, travel across the oceans, the highest mountains and as far and deep underground as desired.

The followers of the Waral way of life acknowledge that the earth doesn't serve mankind, but that mankind serves nature. The Warals acknowledge the underlying truth that nature is exploiting mankind, not the other way around. The Warals respect one major truthful and respectful unique law; One law, One love. This law is represented all around. The diversity of Waral festivities reflect or mirror the diversity of the varying followers of the Waral way of life. One must keep in mind that every festivity and the ones that are yet to come will occur at different times of the year, depending on the local calendar in which the festivities occur. A simple example can be demonstrated when celebrating the seedling or harvesting festival, in the spring on the northern hemisphere and the same festivity occurs six months later on the southern hemisphere. Each festival takes root during a specific time of the year and is celebrated with culinary exchanges, specific imagery , stories and tales related to the festivity. These festivities often result in volunteering such as communication, organisation, construction, preparation and maintenance. These seasonal festivities are not only good opportunities to meet other citizens of the Earth, unite family and friends but they are also a good way to offer help, volunteering for future projects, donating goods and funds to a certain cause or an other. These festivities are also a great opportunity to explore the possible shout outs, also known as direct communication and education.

These festivities are great opportunities to share experiences, thoughts, feelings and passions for diverse projects. Seasonal festivities are an integral part of the calendar of those who follow the Waral way of life. These festivities are representative of the most unique law regarded by the Warals as the only law: One love for humanity, one law of conduct for humanity.

These seasonal festivities, are most often than so, responsible for countless games, songs, myths, stories, activities and enterprises that accompany the celebrations. The list of seasonal festivities grows each passing year. Anyone, of any cultural background, any locality, any sexual orientation, or absence of is encouraged to participate and encourage the creation of any new festivity.

### Festivities and traditions:

Every seasonal festivity is regarded as an important passage from an event and its relationship with the season to next.

January is the festival of the vision. It is focused on the beginning of a new journey, a new season. The festival of the vision can be celebrated by a feast, reading, sharing stories, dinning, music. The festivities in January explore the first vision and personal visions acquired over the ages.

February brings the celebration of the air, and it is coincidently the month of the birth of Charles Darwin, a very influential character in the Waral folklore and legacy. It is also the month of the celebration of Valentinus, former religious figure appropriated by the atheist and pagan cultures. The February festivities are often accompanied by sweets, candy, chocolate, flowers, love letters and other affectionate, and perhaps reproductive behaviours.

March is marked by the spring festival, or the fall festival depending on the location. The northern hemisphere will be more inclined to celebrate the beginning of spring, as the Southern hemisphere will be more inclined to celebrate autumn. In both cases, the March festivities are closely linked to nature. It is the perfect time to prepare seedlings for the garden, or on the contrary, prepare to harvest the fruits of a hard labour.

April is regarded as the festival of the seedlings in the North and the festival of harvest in the South. During this extraordinary succession of events, most followers of the Waral way of life, as well as their guests, enjoy elaborate meals, discuss the seedlings or the harvest respectively of the location of the attendees. The seedlings are transplanted in the gardens, or on the contrary the harvest can finally begin. The beginning of the month is also known as the full eve or the fool's eve.

May, is a month of remembrance and known for the Walkabout festivities. During this month, it is a perfect time to either start or consider a potential walkabout. This month is often celebrated by travels, culinary exchanges, announcements and discussions. The May festivities are focused on the past, present and future walkabouts.

June is regarded as the summer festival in the North, or the winter festival in the South. It can also be interpreted as the celebration of the dry season or the wet season, depending on the location of the attendees. The June festivities revolve around the power of heat, or the power of freezing respectively. Elaborate meals, or on the contrary, light meals are often prepared and served using the fresh produce of the current, or recent season.

August features the festivities of remembrance, specially the relationship that the Warals cultivate between the civilisation of Chelone and the rule of the Dragoons. The August festivities revolve around the history and myths surrounding the Chelonians and the Dragoons. The August celebration, also called the festival of diversity, is commemorated by culinary exchanges coming from different parts of the world, followed by the exchange of local myths and stories.

September brings the fall or autumn festival in the North and the spring festival in the South. In both cases the September festivities are closely linked to nature. It is the perfect time to prepare seedlings for the garden in the South or on the contrary prepare to harvest the fruits of a hard labour in the North.

October contains two important festivities; the festival of the harvest in the North and the festivity of the seedlings in the South. It is also the month of the Feliz gathering. Also known as hollow's eve, or the evening of the dead in some cultures and paradoxically the evening of life in others. The harvest festivities and seedling festivities have been described above. But the Feliz festival is celebrated with decorations, makeup, costumes, discussions and music. Some may want to include sweets, candies and chocolates, others may want to bring out other foods or artefacts. This is a joyous month. The end of the month is also known as hollow's eve and Allô?Ween?

November is regarded as the month of transformation. Some followers of the Waral way of life may honour the transformation of Testudo, Veritix, Mackandal and other characters duly respected by the Warals. The month of November will acknowledge the organic recycling process, also known as transformation or reincarnation by many cultures. This month is viewed as a perfect time for reflection and projection.

December brings the winter festival in the North and the summer festival in the South. The month of December revolves around the success of artisans, artists, scientists, historians and every specialty. The month of December is often celebrated with elaborate culinary exchanges, gifts, songs, stories and the sharing of stories. It is a perfect time to reflect on the importance of personal visions.

## 18 WARALITY IS THE EMBODIMENT OF LIFE, LEVITY, PROSPERITY, CONNECTIVITY, RESPECTABILITY, DIVERSITY AND RESPONSIBILITY.

Passage from Eduardo Ablegado's journal; entry dating from November 21st, 2061 AD. Translated and published by the Scribe of the waters. Original manuscript privately owned by the Ablegado family in Seneta Lusitania. (Published and distributed in April 2063 AD)

Lifestyle and folklore:

Each generation brings a different set of traditions; these traditions inherited and shared across the ages are the result of a strong desire to exchange and discover what appears to be unknown. Curiosity and pursuit of wisdom are incredible driving forces shat should not be ignored. I was only a young child when my uncle left our community. He said he would come back to us after completing an assignment given to him by a strange group of pilgrims known to our family as the walkers. During my uncle's absence, I soon realised that he had chosen to follow the mysterious Waral way of life. From then on I became fascinated by this cryptic and intriguing code of conduct. The sensational humanity guide, the Monitor Codex as well as the epic entitled from "Chelone to Dragoon" had not been published yet. These manuscripts wouldn't be published until years later. The Waral way of life was the source of much gossip in those days. My uncle returned to our community after twelve long years. We were about to celebrate Christmas with him for the first time in what seemed to be a lifetime. I couldn't recognise him. He didn't appear to have aged so much, but the man was definitely not the same as we all remembered. As a child, my uncle was apparently a difficult and rebellious creature. After being involved with somber affairs, fights, excesses and more fights, my uncle decided to change his ways. My uncle, the Walker, brought many gifts for the entire family. This winter, I was finally able to vomit all my questions surrounding the Warals to the point of indigestion.

Almost everything that is known about the traditions and festivities observed by the followers of the Waral way of life comes from accounts of Warals themselves, their friends and their relatives. These historical records and accounts are believed to have been transferred from one Waral scribe to the next. Indeed, every account, every myth, every tradition, every festivity and every historical record is the direct result of Waral scribe's endeavours. So many festivities and traditions have been inherited from one generation to the next. I have concluded that many traditions and festivities closely resemble each other. After an incredible Christmas dinner, I was able to have a chat with my uncle:

"Why do you have dreadlocks?" I asked" Are you a Sadhu? Rastafari? A Druid? A Shaman? A Cree, perhaps?"

"Oh, no. I am something much more ancient than that." he replied. "The term dreadlocks was first coined in the late nineteenth century by a band of cowboys pretending to be soldiers and slave holders. Before that, this hairstyle was known as Jattas, loosely translated from ancient transcript it means; rounded braids. Before that, this hair style was known as snake-like hair during the Hellenistic period. Before that, no one is really sure about the name for the simple reason that this particular hairstyle was adopted by virtually every culture. You see nephew, I have ropes on my head and that is all there is to it. I have chosen to follow the Waral way of life. The Waral way of life is not a religion; it is a code of conduct. The Warals follow a very ethical way of life. The Sadhu are the divine guardians of Shiva, Nama, Rama and many more Brahma divinities. The Sahdus belong to one of the largest religions of the world. They serve their divinities and most, but not all wear Jattas on their heads as a singn of longevity and dedication. Regarding the Rastafari, some orders, or mansions, recognise the last emperor of Ethiopia as a messiah, a divinity and in some cases, he is considered the reincarnation of Jesus, known to the Warals as Keressus, the teacher of Nazareth. Some religious and non-religious alike view Rastafari as a philosophy or an extra step towards religious consciousness. There are countless Rastafari who follow the teaching of the Muslim prophet, others follow Judaic teachings, and some are just interested in the sub culture attached to Rastafari. A large majority of Rastafari do wear Jattas that were later re-defined as dreaded locks, or dreadlocks by those who saw this hair style as a threat. This hairstyle has an incalculable source of meanings. It is believed that in ancient times, for example, only the fiercest captives and gladiators could wear this hair style. Each lock was view as a prowess and a long term commitment. Before that, the old Roman Republic Dictator noted in some of his accounts that this hairstyle was worn by some Gauls and other Germanic tribes. Before these accounts, most of the official records concerning this hairstyle is depicted in art all around the globe. From the cryptic caves in Indonesia, to the most remote European undergrounds, and one must not forget the depictions present in the far East as well as all across the African and American continent. While it is true that most followers of the Waral way of life have hair like mine, we simply call them ropes. You see, nephew, I am a Waral, I have chosen to follow a path driven by science, history and the arts. The Waral way of life doesn't revolve around deities, prophets or dead emperors, no. The Waral way of life revolves around introgressive thinking. The Warals are the record keepers of organic life and of humanity's methods. You see, nephew, the Waral way of life is not a religion, it is a code of conduct.The fact that some of us chose to grow ropes on our heads is simply a way of honouring the past, present and future cultures. Plus, when wearing ropes you no longer lose hair as they are all neatly knit together. And if someone falls into a hole or needs to rescue someone else, one has lots of rope at disposition."

"So, you are trying to tell me that the Warals are an ancient group of historians, and they wear dreadlocks, sorry ropes, as a decorative and security measure?"

"Essentially yes. Those who follow the Waral way of life and decide to grow ropes are ethically bound to be patient individuals."

"Do you wash your hair?"

"Absolutely. The ropes need to stay exceptionally clean in order to remain ropes."

And this is how my uncle and I started to chat about the Waral way of life and all the shrine of mysterious traditions surrounding it. I took notes as he recounted the ancient wars of the armies of stones, the legends of the life of Hatshepsut's favourite garden, the exploits of Yashwanti in Asia. He also told the story of the last giant European lizard killed by the man known as Saint George as well as the letters of warnings believed to have been written by Saint Francis, the pattern of nature. My uncle also talked about the mysteries surrounding the mosquito transformation of Makandal as well as the rumours surrounding the man known to us as Dark Forces who tried to bring an empire down and wished to bring war to a halt. He talked about the American Lion, protector of wild lands, he also mentioned the French Tiger, the incorrigible crime fighter and art lover. I had so many questions, many unanswered. I inquired about the Waral authority and hierarchy. I was also curious about the followers of the Waral way of life's diet and protocols. My uncle was incredibly happy to explain to me that the Warals do not have any central authority and only the peaceful, honest and diverse Waral way of life was able to lead the way. My uncle also explained to me that certain Warals decided to visit or live in dedicated monasteries like educational centres called Sanctuaries. According to my uncle, these Sanctuaries were basically structures that provided quiet and safe surroundings dedicated to the study of mankind's past, present and future. I had always pictured these Sanctuaries as nothing more than libraries in the middle of the woods, inhabited by old gizzards and geeks hiding from the rest of the world. During my childhood and up until my adulthood I always saw the Warals as cowards who refused to be an integral part of society. One day, years after this memorable chat with my uncle, I laid my hands on the "little book of ideas", "the Waral code" and "the Waral histories". As I learned more and more about the Waral way of life, I decided to visit one of these Sanctuaries about which I had heard so much about. Luckily, I was able to discover such a place. My uncle had just risen to the position of scribe in the Sanctuary of the Chocolatine. When I arrived, I was immediately surprised to see the diversity of citizens of the Earth, visiting and residing in the Sanctuary. The place was strategically built on the foot of the Mountain of Mesou, surrounded by the most peaceful parcel of pristine forest. The building was powered by non-intrusive biotechnologies. In fact, I was amazed to see all the dynamos and the turbines tastefully dissimulated in the structure that appeared to be reminiscent of an old European chateau. I was welcomed by my uncle as well as the Monitor of the Sanctuary. My visit was an incredible experience. I discovered the strict lifestyle of those who chose to follow the Waral way of life. For example, I didn't know that, in order to become a Waral, one had to have attained majority. I was also agreeably surprised to see that each individual Waral has individual talents and duties. Every day is driven by an artistic and technological advancement-oriented lifestyle. Each Waral is compelled to learn and teach something new on a daily basis. Most Warals do exercise as an indirect result of their work or hobbies and physical activities. Although some followers of the Waral way of life are not able to, or do not desire to exercise, others have developed an exercise routine. This exercise routine includes running, squat exercises and also a strange type of push-ups. Some Warals refer to these strange push-ups as; sailor's wave push-ups, other have adopted a similar method in which they hold a low push up position. They call this push up exercise; the monitor lizard. The monitor lizard push-ups resemble the posture of a slithering lizard, close to the ground with much force depending on the person's musculature. I was intrigued when I discovered that the Warals do not have any dietary requirements. In general most Warals appear to stay away from junk food and have a real preference for fresh produce. Many observe a vegetarian, or fish-oriented diet; others do eat meat but are not found of fish. Some will eat anything. Each Sanctuary serves breakfast, lunch, goûter around teatime and a copious dinner every single day. The presence of such an incredible variety of meals, appetisers, deserts and other culinary delights compelled me to learn who the chef of the Sanctuary was. It was explained to me that most, if not all Warals, have a natural fondness for growing, raising and cooking their own foods. It appeared that each Waral tended to the gardens and prepared different meals to be shared at the dinner table. Every meal was a banquet for the Warals. Some ate together in the spacious dining room around an enormous table, others brought their portions of foods and drinks to a more secluded and private place. One of the Instructors of the Sanctuary informed me about yearly totems and animals. As it turned out, each follower of the Waral way of life chose a different symbol every year. While some decide to embrace the year of the cat, others identified with the year of the sloth. While some Warals embraced the year of the lizard, or say, the tortoise, others espoused the year of the bat. Some Warals were attached to the African Rooster and kept the bird as a totem year after year. Other Warals kept the Cockerel of Gaul as their totem. This Instructor also informed me that in some cases Warals adopted plants, trees and even minerals as their yearly sign or totem. I will always remember this experience. The Sanctuary was a peaceful, yet animated, place full of knowledgeable citizens of the Earth sharing the same passion for humanity. I was not surprised to learn that Waral births, unions, celebrations and funerals can be conducted by any Waral selected by the group attending the event. At times, some followers of the Waral way of life have been known to conduct ceremonies better than other.

The important element of the Waral way of life is that any walker is able to conduct a celebration as long as the rest of the group attending said celebration agrees. Perhaps the most fascinating aspect of the followers of the Waral way of life is that they all share the same ethical state of mind, which they call Warality. For the Warals, Warality is the embodiment of life, levity, connectivity, respectability, diversity and responsibility.

## 19 A WARAL'S SUMMON AND THE RITUALS ACCOMPANYING IT CAN BE PERFORMED PRIVATELY ALTHOUGH TO SHARE THEM IS NOT UNCOMMON.

Journal of Nmaï the hermit, discovered and translated by the second blue Scribe in the year Alpha zero point zero. Journal privately owned, stored in an undisclosed location in Eastern Asia. (Published in the year Alpha zero point one)

The Earthican Accords:

I always believed that if you want to validate a theory, you must experiment. If the experiment regarding your theory can be conducted more than twice, successfully, then your theory is valid.

Freaks of nature are like perfection; they do not exist. Every entity is different from another. Some entities are so dissimilar from one another than they can appear to look freakish in the eyes of opposed parties. Perfection doesn't evolve, perfection doesn't grow nor shrink. Perfection is so perfect that is doesn't perish, doesn't move and by definition doesn't exist.

The followers of the Waral way of life are by no means perfect innocent gentile beings. We have made many mistakes in the past. Mistakes that we are more than happy to expose in order to heal and move on. Some of the oldest Waral legends expose the brutality, the violence, and the enslavement of entire populations as a result of new territories conquered by the civilisation of Chelone and dominated by the rule of the Dragoons. These accounts obviously underline the genocide, and later the enslavement of Chelonians by the hands of the power hungry Dragoons. The Warals recognise that no population is perfect; no population is innocent and therefore this acknowledgement is the first step that brings us closer as the most forgiving species; humanity. I have remained in total isolation for all these years that I feel that now is the time for me to share my most private Summon and the rituals accompanying it. For a Waral's Summon and the rituals accompanying it can be performed privately although to share them is not uncommon. So let me share something with you, whom ever you are eying my journal! Over the years, I have developed certain rituals to accompany my most private Summon; allowing the fall of the Defendor, also known to us today as the Monster. I forced myself to renounce my life as a hermit. I could no longer afford to remain indifferent to the dictates of the person responsible for so many atrocities. Back then it was illegal to speak against the Monster. My Summon was giving me the strength to trek away from the peaceful and forgotten bog that I once called my refuge. I gathered all my strength, lit the sage, handled my blade and proceeded to shave off my Gandalfic whiskers. I felt it was time to look presentable and rejoin the civilisation that I once belonged to. For months I walked the streets, I shared my hopes for a better world, bad mouthing the ruler of land, risking the repercussions of laisé majesté along the way. Now that he is gone, every Earthican citizen is free to reveal her or his story surrounding the reign of the dictator known as the Defendor.

-Missing pages lost in the fire of Bejerot.-

Most Earthicans were forced to call him the Defendor, but the Warals always referred to him as the Monster. They say the monster was born shortly after the beginning of the twenty-first century. Many stories revolve around his birth, but none of them are clean or flattering. The monster was able to climb the political ladder at such a young age that even the third roman emperor would have been jealous. Once comfortably installed as the president of his country, the monster revealed himself to be an engaging and promising political animal. After a couple of years, his country got involved in proxy conflicts, military interventions, attacks, genocide and ecocides. Eventually the violence escalated into a series of full-blown wars. In the short term, his country was fortunate to gain an immense amount of newly conquered territories. The president and his large country never saw defeat. The man sitting in the presidential palace soon declared martial law to be explicitly imposed on the entire Earthican population. The president soon declared himself as the Defendor of every single Earthican. The newly self-proclaimed dictator was in reality trying to re-establish a Dragoon line. Soon, the Defendor was able to rule the entire globe as a Dragoon Empire, policed and controlled by modern Dragoon regiments, befriending and bribing every ally and crushing every opponent. Soon the dictator elevated his status to Emperor but succumbed to a malady in his middle age. Sickness had infected his twisted mind. As his body recovered, his mental abilities did not. One day during a public speech, the Emperor declared himself the new heir of Ferika, mother of mankind. The Emperor also added the title Monitor of all Warals to his long and pretentious name. This self-proclaimed Defendor of the Earthican Dragon Empire and Monitor of all Warals unleashed so much destruction, wars, pain, violence, nuclear disasters and bio-attacks around the globe that he had to be stopped. The sick and dangerous Emperor was eventually overthrown by some of the most surprising allies. In fact, the Emperor had enraged his own Dragoons. The Monster was pretending to be both the heir of Chelone, the Ruler of the Dragoons as well as the Monitor of all Warals. Rage was also growing amongst the poor Earthican citizens, now dominated by a mad man. As for the Warals, we could no longer remain neutral and distant from such a global urgency. Just like a hundred thousand years ago, during the wars of the armies of stones, and much later during the trades and taming wars, the Warals had to speak up and act. When the failed Emperor was finally deposed, all modern Chelonians, all modern Dragoons and all modern Warals from every nation across the globe agreed to sign the Earthicans Accords. Every single president, prime minister, reagent and state leader of every country was now bounded by the Earthican Accords. The globe was now under the supervision of the Earthican Council, itself presided over by the Head of the Earthican Council. This Accord signed and agreed upon was meant to be a barrier against future wars and most importantly it was a way to protect the globe from any future authoritarian figure. Earthican citizens united behind the same goal; the survival of mankind. After the signing of the Earthican Accord, the old and archaic calendar was dead and the year Alpha zero point zero begun. Every country started to move toward programs that delivered Earthican passports. Traveling became easier, both for business, as well as for pleasure. Global research enterprises could be conducted without limit and an incalculable amount of knowledge, scientific achievements and bio technologies started to flourish. No world exists without conflict and, unfortunately, the year Alpha gave birth to small but violent groups. Two of the most notorious of these groups are the Natural Front and the Mechanics. Both these groups have refused the title of Earthicans. The Mechanics want to rule the skies, while the Natural Front wants to have total control over non-urban areas. Meanwhile, the inhabitants of the civilisation of Chelone as well as the few remaining Dragoon rulers dispatched around the globe have resumed their lives. As for those who, like me, have chosen to follow the path of the Waral way of life, hiding is no longer a necessity.

## 20 ONE BECOMES A WARAL WHEN REFERRED TO AS SUCH BY ANOTHER PERSON. NOT A MOMENT BEFORE.

Passage from Archer's Manual, composed in the early 20th century. Translated by Lurgenn Hoveen and distributed by the Scribe of Quelebs. Original manuscript loaned by the Sanctuary of Letters near Alberta, North America. (First distributed in the year Alpha zero point one)

Re-discovery of the Archer's manual part one. Waral language and communication:

Here I was, digging through books, pamphlets and other ancient manuscripts carefully preserved by the archive department of the famous Alberta Library. I was desperately looking for additional sources of inspiration for my final paper concerning dead languages, cyphers, hidden messages and other obscure dialects. To my surprise, I finally laid my eyes on a very interesting yet mysterious manuscript entitled "the Archer's manual". An incredible source of forgotten knowledge, this book was entirely dedicated to the mode of communication of the followers of the Waral way of life. The Warals, described to me as a discreet group of modern nature worshippers, had their own way of doing things. All I knew at the time was that this peculiar group of individuals had a certain code of conduct that was not very popular at the time. They had strange habits; they had an amazing ability to find each other and to my amazement, the Warals had their own language. I found the Waral's methods of communication absolutely fascinating. And there, I had my subject for my paper:

For starters, a person officially becomes a Waral when referred to as such by an other person, not a moment before. This is probably a way to prevent the self-proclaimed saviours and the likes. It appears that, over time, the followers of the Waral way of life have developed a very simple way to communicate; through simple words, signs, writings, music, dance and other means. The Warals, however, have been simplifying their language down to the simplest form. This simplicity was due to the adjustment and re-adjustment of this almost mystical culture. Additionally, the Waral way of life and its culture had to endure displacement, persecution, genocide, dispersion and finally regrouping. This led to a simple yet effective mode of communication among those who follow the Waral way of life.The most important aspect of the Warals' communication and language directives rely on the intonation, the tempo, the rhythm as well as the quality of the subject of said communication. The modern followers of the Waral way of life make use of only four words. The Warals are also very sensitive to the quality of music or a song as a way to communicate through long distances. For example, most of the music, or songs, played in a minor key are an amazingly effective way to supplement an idea, or an ideal. If a threat must be neutralised, or if a conflict is expected, the quality of the sounds will be delivered in a minor key. However, if a positive event or a celebration is to take place, the music, songs, as well as sounds produced to invite other followers, will be delivered in a major key. The tempo and the rhythm are not negligible attributes of these tunes and songs. Is the event taking place now? Does this event will take place in the future? The tempo and the rhythm will answer these queries. Dances and gestures have two particular impacts, they are visual cues. They communicate the expressions of the message. These visual cues can be understood by those who cannot hear or cannot understand the language spoken. On the cover of the Archer's book was the profile of an archer. The archer was wearing an interesting coiffure; it looked like thick snake-like braids. The bow itself was double bent and the tip of the arrow secured in the indent was serrated. Some passages were in old Norse, others in Inuit. Some passages however were only represented by glyphs and minuscule illustrations. This book, or manual if you will, is one of the most bizarre manuscripts kept in Northern America. Because of my relationship with one of the directors of the collection, I was able to study the Archer's book, or the Waral language and communication manual, in more details than any other linguists or, philologists before me.

Depicted in some of the most ancient archeological sites on the planet, whether on runes, in caves, on stones, tablets, cylinders and other media, the Waral code of conduct and the language that drove its existence for hundreds of thousands of years was reviewing its secrets.

A chick for the birth of a voyage, a bird to drive the voyage, an eye to open the heart and the mind, another bird to find hospitable lands and finally a lion to protect what you cherish so dearly. This was one of the phrases that jumped at me when I finally transcribed the introduction. This obvious Egyptian hieroglyph description was not as innocent as it first appeared to be. In fact, the hieroglyphs of the chick, the bird, the eye, another bird and a lion were depicted many times throughout the manuscript. The same depictions in other runic and glyphic representations were represented over and over again. Was this translation part of a code? Was this a secret message from the author to the reader to decipher? I decided to develop my research. I was to deliver the best paper of my budding career. I soon realised that the Warals tend to bring ideas to life. Their modes of communication breathe with the utmost fluidity. This fluidity is musical in its construction. For example, a form of getting or a simple question is almost always presented as four distinct consonances, it should be noted that my extensive research led me to translate this formal greeting, or question as:

TRE! KTE ! KE ! TEKE !

The response, when describing a positive state of mind, or to describe an event can be noted and translated as:

TAKATA ! KUM ! PA !

If, however, the situation or environment demands a negative response, this can be determined using the first part of the positive reply, using a different tone, followed by a marked silence:

TAKATA ! _ _ _

The Warals have been using this simple mode of communication for ages, it is simple and effective. It could have been catalogued as archaic, primitive and maybe infantile if described two centuries ago. With the existence and the usage of machines and electronics that only communicate using ones and zeroes to form the most complex language and algorithm, I particularly impressed to discover the similarities between the Waral language and our modern computer binary language. After a short period of adaptation, I found myself able to understand, read, speak the ancient language used by the followers of the Waral way of life.

TRE KTE KE TEKE? How are you? How are things?
TAKATA KUMPA Very well, everything is fine.

TRE KTE KE TEKE? What is going on? Are we safe?
TAKATA ! _ _ _Not at all, let's go!

And so on…

## 21 THOSE WHO ARE LEARNING THE WARAL WAY OF LIFE BUT THAT HAVE NOT ATTAINED THE TITLE OF WARAL ARE KNOWN AS HATCHLINGS.

Second passage from Archer's manual. Translated by Lurgenn Hoveen and distributed by the Scribe of Quelebs. (Year Alpha zero point one)

Archer Manual part deux.

The Archer Manual piqued my interest for the simple reason that it also introduces the reader to a mysterious musical code, an early version of sheet music perhaps? Certain design appeared to represent a major scale, it was decorated with bright colours, flowering plants, little creatures and humans dancing. A second illustration was seemed to be the representation of a minor scale. It was a gloomy representation accompanied by dark motifs as well as shrivelling plants and a few skeletal remains. A third illustration, my personal favourite, was the representation of both scales intertwined in a sensational marriage of flesh, life, death and completion. The most striking feature of this third illustration was that both scales appeared to merge at the bottom of the illustration as much as in the top of this beautiful design. A fourth and final music illustration representing another arrangement that appeared to be switching from a major to a minor scale. This was interesting and I was sure that this discovery would interest some of the most renowned musicologists. But it did not. It was the next part of the book of Archer that most were fascinated with. The next segment of the manuscript was indeed a lesson in rhythms and the magical attributes behind the subtle usage of tempo. The usage of music, rhythms and their different tempos is a global phenomenon. It is easy to recognise the similar progressions used by different cultures separated by thousands of miles and yet all these rhythms and musicality rely on the same point of origin. Most rhythms described in the book of Archer are somehow closely related to both the old world as well as the new world. Independent of human's disparity and migrations, these rhythms and tempos appeared to have traveled much faster than their proper authors or creators. Music, cultures, languages and adaptational needs are in essence all linked by the perception of our senses. Did the ancient Warals know about the spectacularly fast migration of cultural habits? Were the followers of the Waral way of life at the origin of this extraordinary cultural migration? Did the Warals import and export cultural habits for the benefit of the incredible human migration? I was never able to provide any solid evidence, but I am now convinced that the Warals have a strict penchant for remaining in the shadows. As one passage of the book of Archer tells; the Warals, as fond of literature and education as they may appear to be, never desired to inscribe the cultural heritage of the Waral way of life in one single book. The followers of the Waral way of life have always been advocates of multiple sources of knowledge; they did not wish to create a manuscript relieving all the Waral secrets and traditions. The Waral much preferred to have different literary notices and accounts acknowledging their existence; for the ancient Warals that was sufficient. The ancient Warlas were referenced in the far East during the expansion of the empire of the great Khan. The Warals had a small place within Egyptian folklore as well as in the early accounts describing the debaucheries of Enkidu. The followers of the Waral way of life appeared to have been in contact or perhaps part of virtually all cultures, old and new. Could a modern Waral help me decode and translate the book of Archer? No. I had to find a Waral with a desire to work for endless hours, a Waral with no particular mission or assignment, a Waral with no attachment or responsibility toward a Sanctuary. Hell, this research quickly turned into hell. I was never able to find a Waral to help me decipher this mysterious manual. I had to present my paper; so I did. It was an incomplete translation of the book of Archer. I had to present a small portion of a great discovery. I had worked for months and did have to introduce the Waral langue and its other musical modes of communication. After a theatrical presentation in front of a skeptical audience, my heart almost walked out of my chest. My research was poorly received by the class and the faculty. This was the day I decided to pursue a career, not in linguistics, but in anthropology and mythology. When, a year later, I presented a paper remarkably similar to the one presented a year before, the response was not negligible. My class-mates as well as the professor pushed me to continue my research; I soon focused exclusively on the Waral way of life language and their mysterious folkloric traditions.

I was compelled to differentiate and then compare different modern cultures that share similar attributes. These attributes have been inherited for generations. These attributes sometimes give the impression that they took root in a more ancient and different culture. There are many examples that can be demonstrated, but the most notable are embedded in traditional music and ceremonial or celebratory dances. When analysing certain songs and dance moves one cannot help but notice the exact same construction across diverse cultures. As I travelled to the northern plains of America, as I adventured myself on the shores of Armoric Brittany and when I was welcome to participate in a celebration of the new season on the immense Mongolian terrain, I took many notes, recorded as many songs and arrangements as possible. I gathered pieces of a global puzzle; each piece connected to the next. After spending years collecting my data it was finally time to file my findings and discover the links between all these incredible traditional songs and dances. I was fortunate enough to ask some of my musician friends as well as some of my dancer friends to look at a few pieces of evidence. The amazing thing happened. My results proved a very ancestral link between all these notes, rhythms and notes. A striking resemblance could be drawn between the way different cultures separated from each other geographically but also living during different times. This gave homage to the sun or in some cases to a sun deity. When comparing what is commonly called the "sun dance", performed by different folklores, it is extraordinarily reassuring to note that the introductory moves, as well as the different rhythm patterns can be identified with certitude, no matter where or when the culture made use of these " sun dance" moves. It appears that some cultures are more inclined to preserve their heritage than others. This heritage can be expressed by art, technologies, common folkloric beliefs, traditional methods as well as diverse codes of conduct. What compels a culture to preserve its ancestral traditions? The result of persecution? The desire to remain attached to the past? Or simply because some cultures are just too beautiful to disappear. Some cultures can perish, be buried under layers of lies, forgotten and finally revived. There are many examples of revived or what could be catalogued as "resurrected" cultures. While some cultures survive far from the eyes of our modern Earthican civilisation, one element deserves to be noted.

Some cultures desire to remain hidden, some cultures are forced to remain hidden and other cultures rarely interact with other communities. These rare interactions do not allow outsiders to really study these cultures. The final noteworthy element is that new cultures are born every day, some endure through the ages and some exist in a series of events determined to imitate or honour a certain culture. Some cultures are based around real events, sometimes based on entertainment, but these cultures make us who and what we are. When cultures are confronted with one another they either merge into one or cohabit side by side. This cohabitation can be achieved peacefully or not; this cohabitation can be achieved independent of geographical needs and distances. The Warals have been studying different cultures and approaches of millennia. As a result, the followers of the Waral way of life have a deep understanding of the need to immerse oneself in a culture, study it and discover links with another. The Waral practice the introgressive method as a way to secure continuity. This continuity concerns the accumulation of ancient and modern knowledge in order to have a minimum of material to prepare for the future. The links between organic materials as well as the links between methods and ideas are the main focus of the followers of the Waral way of life. Those individuals not recognised as Warals, for either reason, are known as Hatchlings. This is a reference to the first article of the chart of Aukhaun that states : Those who are learning the Waral way of life but that have not attained the title of Waral are known as Hatchlings. These Hatchlings are the learners, the young and individuals who haven't been named a Waral by an other. A fascinating aspect of the followers of the Waral way of life is that the name of their group as well as a non-negligible amount of their habits have been referenced and noted in virtually every culture on the planet. Many runes, scripts, inscriptions and documents lead to the conclusion that the Warals have been present among us for as long as humanity can be recorded. All cultures point out the existence and the perseverance of the Waral way of life.

The Nubians, Carthaginians, Gauls, Germanic Tribes, Norse, Russ, Babylonians, Assyrians, Akans, Ocenaitians, Abyssinians, Olmec, Greco Roman, the inhabitants of the forest named the "Hoo I Ahh", etc. All these geographically and temporarily separate cultures have mentioned the existence of the followers of the Waral way of life.

For example, the inhabitants of the Eastern Crescent note the word Waral as 'a flat trident to trace the road, a slit to represent the skies, a V for connectivity, another slit to represent the skies and an upside down V or hat to complete and protect the journey'.

Coincidently the inhabitants of northern Nubia depicted the Warals as chick, a bird, an eye, another bird and a lion.

Another example can be observed in the book of Rudolph as the flowering line accompanied by the famous plunging nymphs.

The followers of the Waral way of life, the bridge between the natural and mechanical world and they have left clues all over the globe. The Warals have left their mark across distances, cultures, localities and have survived through an extraordinary succession of kingdoms, territories, empires, dominions, republics and other unnamed legislative governments. The Warals have been taming the wildest creatures and sharing their most outrageous views and methods to any interested parties across the ages. The Warals are, messengers of the skies, thanks to their carrier birds. The Warals are, in charge of the most delicate missions, in charge of sending messages securely fastened to their three prong arrows to notify allies and warn off enemies. The Waral language, its musical mode of communication as well as all its depictions was to be the focus of my career as a professor. Eventually, I met some of the most astute students who, at least for one of them, showed me that I had yet to discover many more Waral secrets and songs. Of all the Waral songs, four of them deserve to be explored in more details. These four elemental songs about the air, water, fire and the earth respectably cannot be denied as they have entered our modern musical lexicon.

'The Wind' was a song focused on the aerial elements. 'The Wind' was originally a song in French later translating into English a bit before the passage to the year Alpha zero point zero. The original song was about the wind devouring an entire village. The next adaptation of the song focused on the power of the wind itself. A later interpretation was viewed as a struggle against the frozen manners of a wintery turbulence. This song is still played today by Warals and non-Warals alike. The song is traditionally played in E minor It goes something like this: four beats in E minor, four beats in C, four beats in A, two beats in G and two beats in G diminished putting the accent on the note G becoming F#. Would you like to know the words? Here we go:

The wind:

Ca c'est ta saison, ca c'est notre saison, ca c'est sa saison, ca c'est ma saison, ca c'est notre saison.

Le vent s'engouffrait sous les murs, temperature du clair obscure

Bourrasque venue de nulle part, violent tourbillon glacial

Bise de passage, souffle du carnage

Une halte, un moment de repis

Je sortais découvrir les restes de mon domaine

Le mecontantement de mere nature vous a retirer tout espoir de naitre.

Un grabuge plus que rafraichissant vous a retirer tout espoir de naitre.

La Batailla del Fuego is an other popular song. It is a rhythmic composition: trekteketeke takata kumpa trekteketeke takata.

An-other interesting song is that of The Nile. This song has a traditional footing entrenched in Em for two beats, then one beat in G and an other in A. It is said that an occasional descent from C to B occurs, depending on the interpretation.

The Nile:

I was born deep inside a termite mound, slithering my way up the River Nile.

Watching the sky high, flicking my tongue at everything that moves. Just a few miles from the nearest feast.

I just monitor the Nile. Watch me! Waral survive! I just monitor the Nile; they want me dead or alive.

Time for happy hour, look! Here's a carcass in the water. Good, good, good, good, carrion. Flicking my tongue at everything that moves. Just a few miles from the nearest feast.

I just monitor the Nile. Watch me, while I survive. I just monitor the Nile. They want to use me dead or alive.

Time for happy hour again. Here's an other carcass in the water. Good, good, good, good carrion. Flicking my tongue at everything that moves. Just a few miles from the nearest feast.

I just monitor the Nile. Watch me! Waral survive! I just monitor the Nile, they want me dead or alive.

An-other interesting composition, a chant without instruments, is entitled Terra Nova or Terra Novae depending on the interpretation.

Terra Nova/Terra Novae:

Terra A. Terra volubilis, terra A. Terra A.

Terra matter ante, terra A.

Radix est, radix est a terra A. Radix est.

Terra matter, terra A. Terra A.

Elementanio terra A. Terra matter.

Terra A. Terra volubilis, terra A. Anteniro da. Terra A.

Terra matter, terra A.

# III Propagation:

When Nöel, Les and I arrived in Washington D.C. to operate, we met with Governor Celine Mare and her District Attorney Josh Derigher. Les and Derigher had dealings with each other in the past. Despite his reputation as a racist and a homophobe, Josh Derigher had built his own political machine centred on social acceptance. Without going into further details, all I can say is that Josh Deringher used photo ops and P. R. like a famished, political shark. The man was lying and plotting on every occasion that presented itself. The fact that a person of this nature can hold on to a post as a government official in our day and age is totally beyond me. Some would argue that this is due to the power of money, some say it is the power of charisma and others frankly do not care. Noël and I knew the newly elected Governor of Washington D. C. very well. My old friend referred to the Governor as "Madame Maire" and I simply called her Governor Celine Mare. We all met at the Governor's mansion. Josh Derigher was waiting for us outside the main entrance of the building. As he watched us approaching the gates Josh shouted:

"Hey, isn't it my old pal' General Roken and his geeky lil' friends. Glad you are here; we got a big job for you guys!"

"Oh, my globe!", said Noël," check it out! The Governor's Bichon Frisé is on the loose! Look out, he bites!"

I had to calm the game; I remember saying with a soft voice:

"Gentlemen please, let us behave like civilised Earthicans. A catastrophe is unfolding as we speak. We can always quarrel later."

Nöel, Les and I walked closer to the main door; Josh was now leaning on the door frame. The devious bastard looked right at me with a smile and remarked:

"Oh, Sam, you are so adorable, as usual". He glanced at Les for a moment, turned his attention back to me and continued. "So, you and Les? Tell me Sam, are you still sucking the general's chocolate mars bar? "

(Pook! Boom! Flat!) The DA's nose broke.

Against my better judgment it seems that my forehead had taken the initiative of smashing the Governor's DA right in the middle of the face. I soon realised that Josh Derigher was bleeding heavily. My impolite victim was in desperate need of a tissue that I was only very happy to provide. I wiped my naughty forehead, handed him the tissue and apologised:

"Sorry mate, my noggin has a mind of its own. Oh, and by the way, yes Josh, I'm still sucking my lover's enormous chocolate mars bar."

"My nose, he...you...ouch...he broke my fucking nose!" cried Josh.

I turned to Noël and said, "Right so, let's get to work. We have important decisions to make and tons of paperwork to fill."

The Governor shouted across the corridor:

"Sam, Noël, General Roken! I'm so happy you are here. Follow me this way into the conference room." We all followed the Governor while she unraveled the situation to us: "D.C. is totally infested with this plant. Oh, and I must apologise for Josh's foul mouth." She looked at me with a grin accompanied by two thumbs up and whispered, " Nice!"

Derigher was still recuperating and moaning in the main hall. He was keeping his head backwards to stop the bleeding while the rest of us finally stepped into the conference room leaving him alone in the corridor.

"I'm fine," said Josh," I'll be fine... just start with... ouch, fuck.... just start without me; I'll join you in a sec'."

After a long, painful talk about tactics and logistics, we signed all the necessary documents and agreements and the Governor escorted us to our vehicle, which was parked right outside the mansion. Before we drove off, she gave us a piece of friendly advice:

"You guys are our only hope, for now. But I felt I had to tell you that competition is fierce out there. My intel confirmed that our government is, as we speak, trying to surpass your services. The Anti Bioterrorism and Bio-threats Agency, your agency, will always be our favourite agency to go to when the shit hits the fan. But we may receive estimates and proposals soon. Just letting you know."

"Understood ma'am', thank you ma'am'" said Les.

"I just felt like telling you," said the Governor. "Good luck, you guys, D. C. is in your hands now."

"Merci, Madame Maire," said Noël. "No pressure at all!"

Les, Noël and I climbed back into the car. I could not help myself and shouted through the open window:

"Laters', my darlings. Sorry Josh!"

As we drove away from the Governor's home, I spotted something peculiar in the distance. A group of individuals dressed up like monks were observing our departure from the Governor's mansion. They were staying close to the edge of the forest. This view was strange enough for me to remember, but I did not think anything of it at the time; I was distracted as my wrist screen was now bombarding me with news flashes and correspondences. Noël, on the other hand, was now plunged into his old school, paper map of DC.

We soon intervened in D.C., then we moved on to the next infected area in Maryland, then back in the direction of Northern Virginia and so on. Meanwhile we heard on the news that the Mechanics had just deployed four additional stations on Mars. The Mechanics had just launched an attack on one of the Earth's most important ports, resulting in bloodshed and an incredible financial mess. The Mechanics organisation was targeting different countries' economies in order to reignite international conflicts. The obvious goal of the Mechanics was to put an end to the Earthican Accords. Their aim was to divide humanity once more in the hopes of perhaps one day claiming Earth as their own. Our modern world has matured over the years. The Earthican Accords is the only thing protecting governments and regencies from waging wars like the days of old. The Earthican Accords have united all nations against the Mechanics. In other news, on the other side of the globe, the Natural Front was detaining a handful of diplomats. The Natural Front was collecting hostages from all over the globe in order to extort local and international governments. They were exercising a tremendous amount of pressure on the Earthican Council. The Natural Front was determined to use terrorism to reclaim and control our planet's precious natural resources. Because the Mechanics lived in orbit and because the Natural Front was operating in the shadows, the minds of certain Earthican citizens started to gravitate towards conspiracy theories. Some bloggers and books were trying to deny the existence of the Mechanics, they even denied the existence of the Natural Front. These sources claimed that all the darkness and terror of the world was a direct result of the Warals' desire to rule the world. The followers of the Waral way of life have been described as a sort of occult sect focusing on the study of virulent poisons and mystical spells. Some of these conspiracy theorists viewed the Warals as devil worshippers; they viewed the followers of the Waral way of life as some sort of antichrist society getting ready to dominate mankind. There was absolutely no proof of that, but these books and articles proved to be immensely popular and marketable. Since the Mechanics and the Natural Front were operating in the shadows, the curious and imaginative crowds turn to the Warals in order to unite against a common and quite visible enemy.

The Anti-Bioterrorism and Bio-threat agency worked relentlessly for months. The rule of terror of this poisonous plant finally came to an end when winter came. I must admit that our success was in part due to the mobilisation and awareness of the general population. Every Earthican citizen, from different economic backgrounds, from different localities and different beliefs had united in helping prevent the dispersion of the freakish plant. And as for the removal of the plant itself, in infected areas, our Agency found some of the most surprising allies. Indeed, from local fire departments to various pleasing and police forces. We also received great manpower with the assistance of ordinary and extraordinary volunteers, including civilians as well as newly formed organisations inspired by our agency's methods. Some of these organisations are now considered promising partners and yet possible future competitors. It is quite flattering that our agency has reached a point that is encourages cooperation through competition. Every entity has a specialty after all. The beauty of our modern society is the acknowledgement of similarities, but at the same time it is driven by an admiration for our individual differences. But unfortunately, a society without crime would not be able to endure. Since this toxic plant started to appear all over the globe, the news has been focusing on reports of gangs and black-market leaders getting involved with eradication operations for the right price. One news article, written by Noël's girlfriend Judith was entitled "Crime doesn't pay, much". The article underlined the plant's devastative effects on the grey economy. It also exposed the direct repercussions on the most despicable criminal organisations. One anonymous mob boss was quoted saying: "We had to intervene and even help the cops getting rid of that plant, you know, off the books. That thing was literally and figuratively killing both our profits and our future customers."

This individual was referring to the plants' ability to render sterile any person exposed to its toxic pollen. The article "Crime doesn't pay, much" was the journalistic break Judith was waiting for. In fact, it was the year her journalistic career really took off! One might say that this article propelled her to the top of the news business. Her subsequent articles ; " A.B.B.A the agency that we have all been waiting for" and "Eradication of the plant done, with winter's help" quickly changed her financial situation as well as her lifestyle.

I cannot stress that enough, but at some point, Noël and I did consider resigning from the agency. It was in late December; the year was Alpha six point one. All the members of the Anti-Bioterrorism and Bio-threat Agency as well as their families had gathered to celebrate new year. We also celebrated our victory over the toxic plant. We all thought that the worse was behind us. After all, it was our little custom to unite every year to celebrate our achievements of the year. This time it was different. Noël and Judith had slowly grown apart. Judith wanted to pursue an international career in journalism; she also developed a lavish lifestyle in a noticeably short period of time. My old friend Noël's only desire was to settle down. He wanted to leave the agency and focus on his passion for anthropology, sociology and the history of the Waral way of life. Noël wanted to be the first to translate and publish what he called; the Waral code. I noticed that there was something else drawing a deep wedge between Judith and my old friend Noël. It was something that I would not discover until much later. New Year's Eve was unfolding as planned; we had plenty of food, plenty of drinks, magic cigarettes for the adults, tons of presents and cake for the kids. On this night, Les and I announced our engagement. We announced our plans to get married and start a family of our own. We informed our friends that we were looking to get a large house with a garden and plenty of space to raise kids. This was to be an exciting new chapter in our lives. Everyone at the party was enchanted; this was the highlight of the soirée. Babs had just celebrated her seventy-first birthday and she was more vigorous than ever. She was remarkably close to Zed. Babs and I hoped that our young protege Zed would one day replace Mammy Kitty. Zed was having lots of fun playing with Babs and her grandchildren. The security team had a laugh reminiscing about their old assignments while their respective partners exchanged pleasantries. Mehdi was playing music for everybody. This year he brought his Oud, a string instrument. It is a sort of a middle eastern lute. The young man was singing one of his favourite songs called "Araya" and almost everybody was clapping their hands. Some of us were dancing and others were simply relaxing. On this night, the atmosphere was appeasing. It was pleasant to let go after such a disastrous year. Millions of Earthicans had been infected in less than a year and the economy was going down the drain. But on this night, most of us had a pinch of hope in our hearts.

I truly believe that that was the last time I saw Noël pretending to be happy. None of us could image what was going to happen next. Little did I know, this was to be the last soirée attended by the original forming members of the Anti-Bioterrorism and Bio-threat Agency. I could sense that Nöel was not doing so well that night. I always knew that talking about feelings and intimate thoughts always made my old friend uncomfortable, but I was determined to figure out what was the matter with him. With the courage of a pint of chilled lagger and accompanied by the power of my heart, I finally asked Noël:

'Nice evening, innit?

"I guess so" he replied.

"Noël, we did it. This feckin' plant head ache thing is over. Cheer up, mate!"

"Listen Sam, I think I'm done. I need to get away from all of this. You, Les, Zed, Babs, Mehdi and the team don't need my help anymore. I think I need to move on and finish my book."

"You just want to finish this Waral code project of yours, am I right?"

"Well yes, the Waral code isn't going to write itself. I have a lot of work to do; my research isn't over yet. And, look, I don't really care if I write the worst book in history, but the Waral code needs to be written."

"I, I understand." As I heard these words coming out of my mouth I suddenly realised that I actually did not understand so I added: " This type of research must be a bit like studying ancient Rome, ancient Egypt or Mesopotamia, right?" I couldn't anticipate his infuriated response:

"Fuck ancient Rome! Fuck ancient Egypt and fuck ancient Mesopotamia!" screamed Noël. "These are baby civilisations compared to the Waral heritage! Putin de bordel de merde; you still don't understand, do you?

The Warals have been walking across the globe for at least a hundred thousand years and they are still walking among us today. The Warals live by a code that has never been compiled into a single volume. I have tons of clues and tiny fragments of clues that I have to translate from languages that haven't been spoken in ages. The Warals are not isolated individuals on the margin of society. They help create new societies. Their history deserves all my attention now."

I sensed that my old friend was in need of comfort, I apologised for my remark leading to his outburst. It was my fault; I knew he was very sensitive about the subject. In turn, my old friend apologised for raising his voice and noted that my initial inquiry was pertinent indeed. Noël seemed troubled and distracted. To me, the Waral way of life was just a concept at the time. To me the Warals represented a shadowy group of nature-worshiping pilgrims that only desire to remain on the fringes of society. Noël, on the other hand, was profoundly fascinated by them. I can distinctly recall that when we were both students in Northern New Gaul, a life time ago, he was already talking about the Warals and their fantastic affinities with the laws of nature. His obsession for the Waral way of life eventually faded after he realised that there is no more room for poetic ideals in our modern society. My old friend came to terms with the fact that our modern world is now ruled by the Earthican Council. Our modern world may appear to be united on the surface, but it is still subjected to conflicts between governmental and ideological ideals. I cannot describe the horrors instigated by the Mechanics orbiting our precious globe and the Natural Front hiding in remote forests here on Earth. These two extremist groups are at each other's throats. Each year, thousands of civilians are caught between the interminable conflicts between them. The Mechanics live in the heavens; they are untouchable while the Natural Front is invisible, but they still manage to shed blood, too much blood. Our modern world gives the appearance of peace and unity, but conflicts are still raging out there. My old friend Noël once told me that our modern world no longer has any interest in those who voice an affinity for poetry and responsibility. He also told me that our modern world was no longer welcoming those who follow the Waral way of life and that was killing him inside.

## 22 A WARAL MAY BE GIVEN OR CHOOSE MANY TOTEMS OR SIGNS. BUT ONLY ONE WILL GIVE AWAY ITS SECRETS TO A WARAL.

Passage from the log of the Earthican Waral Association recorded by the pink Scribe, translated by Hu Kyuan Ling. Manuscript privately owned, stored in an undisclosed location near the Korean basin. (Published in the year Alpha zero point one)

Admixture: a bright future for the followers of the Waral way of life:

After the agreements and signings of the Earthican Accords, the Warals had no other option but to become officially recognised. As the path towards Warality is not a religious path but an ethical and philosophical path driven by history and science, some followers of the Waral way of life started to build Sanctuaries with nonprofit-oriented structures in order to provide educational, scientific and historical teachings. Some establishments also provided a residence for the followers of the Waral way of life. These Sanctuaries were soon classified, unofficially, as places of worship. Places for individuals with a need to worship education, ethics, science, history, the arts, agronomy and so on. The aftereffects of the Earthican Accords gave birth to a new fascination for cultural and folkloric heritage. Indeed, citizens from all over the globe were finally able to travel to unknown destinations. The most isolated, curious minds living on remote islands were able to visit the great modern capitals of the world; in turn some of the most urban citizens had finally the occasion to visit all the exotic places they could only dream of visiting only a few years earlier. The creation of this multicultural Earthican Council allowed local and international agencies to prosper and partner up. Of course, no civilisation can exist without crime. No world can survive if it pretends to desire to look like a unicorn rainbow land were all the chocolate bears are holding hands. The Earthican Accord may have killed wars and other international conflicts. All the Earthen citizens living under the same roof, our planet. Crime and violence were still a remnant of humanity's animalistic nature, or it was perhaps a simple way to demarcate ourselves from the savage, yet predictable existence that is the natural world. Yes, human nature was the only true untameable force. Human nature was and still is a secret and forgotten taboo exploited every single day for everyone to see. What a paradoxical existence, yet this existence is our own. We must own it and be responsible about it. As humans have been using other humans; nobody can say for sure which population was the first to practice slavery, serfdom and other atrocious actions towards members of our own species. These monstrous actions had to provoke some level of discomfort and shame. This is why humans have always loved to patronise other cultures or on the contrary have persisted again and again, to ignore some of their own actions. As the Earthican Accords gave birth to a new and connected society, it also gave rise to dangerous groups, fragmented from reality. I am speaking of course of the Natural front and the

Mechanics. These small fractions started as simple associations of conspiracy theorists. The problem is that both organisations, as different as they may have appeared, had the exact same mode of operation. Their methods relied upon terror, bribery and subtle associations with some of the most despicable individuals on the planet. While the Natural Front displaced entire populations to confiscate lands and establish their own territories, the mechanics did the exact same thing, but their aim was the skies. Infiltration of different space programs, stealing plans from the brightest aero engineers and acquiring enough resources, they finally conquered the Earth's atmosphere. At first, they just boarded stations and expelled their occupants in shuttles to simply fly them back home. They eventually switched to a darker method. The mechanics would simply board new space stations and facilities and just killed anything or anyone along the way. They soon stopped to spare life all together. The future was looking bright on Earth. The economy was up. The environment was no longer something to protect or exploit but became an integral part of our modern natural and mechanical world. Indeed, the Earthican population has taken the time to understand and appreciate its surroundings. Trash became a source of energy, Natural disasters were now simply avoided using nature itself as a shield, like all the mangroves and swamps re-established in areas sensitive to floods, tsunamis and other disastrous cyclones. Security measures were taking a different turn with the creation of the Please Force and the Environmental Assistance Programs. And since the end of formal global Conflicts, the emergence and businesses based on preventive equipment has been booming. Nicknamed "non-lethal weapons," these pieces of equipment are so sophisticated than some model can disable old school guns using a magnetic technology that renders the most dramatic automatic rifle to the most discrete handgun totally useless. Due to this magnetic technology, the bullet and other projectiles are able to be protected even if the weapon itself it activated or detonated. An amazing defence mechanism has been introduced via auditory waves. These sonic pieces of equipment can cause a great deal of damage, but they do not kill. A slew of big companies has also developed anti detonation devices. These devices are able to dismantle gorilla style cocktails and ultra-advanced mechanisms alike. As mentioned previously, the world may be a better and safer place, but darkness is always lurking within humanity's achievements, as beautiful as they are. Crime is and will, unfortunately, always thrive. The good news is that our modern Earthican government is making things pretty difficult for criminals. Some groups have been focusing on bio-terrorism. Some of these groups have been successful in their attempts to destabilise or control local government. This had been an ongoing problem for a while now. But luckily, one organisation soon emerged as a global emblem for unity, strength, determination and responsibility against bio-terrorism and other organically disrespectful groups. This organisation, called the Anti-Bioterrorism and Biothreat Agency, was dominating the media and the imagination of the Earthican population. This Agency managed to put an end to the proliferation of the killer algae, Taxipholia, in the Mediterranean and along the American east coast. It's the same agency which was responsible for stopping the spread of air borne diseases, invasive species and other virulent natural and man plagues around the globe. This organisation is known worldwide as A.B.B.A. The two owners of the Agency have appeared on our little home screens and on our wrist screens. Their faces were all over the news for the longest time. One of the two is a tall, skinny red-headed, an anthropologist or historian of some repute and the other looks like a short and chubby mad professor; the cameras love them! These two and their team have been the source of merchandise, books and documentary programs. This Agency is the first governmental entity to have attained an almost lovable status among local populations. I think is it because they do not work with humans, but they work with plants, animals and organisms that most are unable to work with. A few years ago, it was announced that the Anti-Bioterrorism and Biothreat Agency would one day develop an air born laboratory. I can't wait to see what kind of contraption they will come up with. It must be noted that one of the owners of this Agency, the tall red-headed one, is familiar with our Waral way of life. It is probably wise to say that we should perhaps keep an eye on his future discoveries. I only mention it in this log as he is clearly aware that a Waral may be given or choose many totems or signs. But only one will give away its secrets to a Waral. These words came out of his own mouth during an interview. How could he known about this? And why would the use or misuse of totems matter to him? I do not know.

## 23 THE WARAL WAY IS ABSOLUTELY AGAINST PREJUDICE AND DISCRIMINATION.

Passage from "The one term seeker, new head of the Earthican Council". Article composed by the Scribe of the marshes and published by the Earthican gazette. (Published on May 4th of the year Alpha zero point two)

The one term seeker:

Every Sanctuary teaches about The One Term seeker these days. It is hard to pass around the legends surrounding The One Term seeker's administrative and legislative achievements. As soon as the Earthican

Accords were signed, every head of state offered to be the head of the newly formed global government; the Earthican Council. The Earthican Council was to be presided, directed and driven by whoever was declared as The Head of the Earthican Council. Competition was fierce, like any political environment; the race to become Head of the Earthican Council led to a series of alliances and rude competition. As announced by the legislative committee, the Head of the Council was authorised to accumulate three consecutive terms. The One Term Seeker was a very notable Head of the Council because she accomplished all her promises in one term and retired from the post without seeking a second, nor a third term. The One Term seeker happened to have been a follower of the Waral way of life. At first nobody cared, but when she was elected the first female Head of the Earthican Council, she started to open up about it. None of us Warals had any prior knowledge of the Head of the Council's devotion for the Waral way of life. It was a valuable lesson for all of us, Warals or not. During her campaign, all the public was interested about was her extraordinary and adventurous background. Born in Senegal, youngest economics teacher at the University of Dakar, she eventually became the ambassador of Ukraine, helped creating micro universities, micro hospitals and health clinics in South America, notably in the Amazon basin area and other remote locations. Anita Timouole had become a sensational phenomenon. Her career as a politician, a professor of economics and as a philanthropist contrasted with that of her opponents. The fact is that policies change over time, but politics do not. Most of her opponents had a typical bureaucratic or military curriculum vitae under their belts. Most of them had been presidents or leaders of their own countries, most of them had been involved in some of the most grotesque affairs, the type that buzz around ordinary politicians like flies negotiating a landing on someone else's cake. Anita was truly a fresh political figure with nerves of steel. She outsmarted the other nominees; she devoted as much time to her voters as to her critics. The most outrageous legislations were passed during her first and only term. As she once famously said in a live speech:

"We cannot ignore human nature; we can no longer afford to turn a blind eye. The necessity for pleasure and violence is part of human nature. We must allow ourselves to harvest the fruits of our nature. After all, mankind doesn't need more food, it is in dire need of contraception and protective measures. Mankind is in dire need of liberty and freedom of expression. Let us not forget what the Romans did for entertainment; they had the games. Let's not forget our great grandparents obsessions with gore movies and violent sports. Let us not forget that some of us do not find violence as pleasurable as others. Let us turn our backs against prejudice. As most of you know, I follow the path of the Waral way of life, and I am absolutely against prejudice and discrimination. Let us embrace our localities, our backgrounds, our sexual orientations as well as our freedom of expression. Let us embrace human nature. Peaceful and benevolent humans also deserve to blow off some steam. We are all Earthican citizens; every individual deserves liberty, security and entertainment. No matter how peaceful, no matter how violent, every individual has the right to choose the source and type of entertainment she or he wishes to enjoy. My fellow Earthicans; I am a candidate. I intend to win and when I do, will sit with the council as the Head of the Earthican Council I will make sure that not a single pleasure or liberty will be condemned."

The One Term seeker was putting an accent on the undeniable truth that vices are more profitable than virtues. In other words, when the first female Head of the Earthican Council, a self-proclaimed one term seeker, legalised all drugs and all pleasure houses, including some of the most despicable establishments, the economy boomed overnight and violence plunged the next day. The first year of the One Term Seeker as Head of the Earthican Council was a very controversial period of adjustment for every single Earthican citizen. The most conservative groups criticised the lack of manners and lifestyle that these new laws generated. On the other side of the spectrum, some liberal entities were outrage because of the new terms "pleasure workers" had replaced the ancestral term "sex workers". The leather industry and its colourful customers were enchanted by this bold move, not made by a mere head of state, but by the first female Head of the Earthican Council. Indeed, pleasure houses, bath houses, massage houses, kinky bars, leather galleries and naturist retreats were in essence, becoming in vogue, in a classy, safe, and most importantly, commercial way. As for the drug stores, they kept the same name, but changed their inventories in order to include actual drugs. Some of these substances were classical synthetic narcotics; other products were directly derived from natural sources and as a repercussion, most gardening stores, florists and farmers started to expand their productions and their goods. Because of the uproar surrounding these new legislative and economical exploits, the Earthican government had to be on top of its game now. There was a new attention to awareness programs, safe environments, controlled products, intricate waivers to sign before entering bdsm clubs and other drug dens. By making the clients, and the customers, aware of the risks in an objective fashion, this new pleasure and violence industry had gained a somewhat valid reputation. Indeed, after visiting one of the greatest fetish establishments in Washington D. C. I can testify that all kinky activities were conducted with the most respectful and consensual manner. As for the drug establishments, I can only speculate and repeat what I've seen on my little home screen or from what I heard from a colleague a while ago. These drug houses are apparently quite clean and focused solemnly on product quality and health protocols. As the Head of the Earthican Council, Anita managed to drive the world economy up. She also made the population realise its own tastes for such pleasures and she also managed to initiate the "wild routes," a series of environmentally secured pathways only accessible to wildlife, scientists as well as conservators. As the world has become more connected than ever, in part due to the repercussions of the Earthican Accord, trade, imports and exports became the easiest form of commerce. No more conflicts and wars of terror to slow down the flow of economic and cultural exchanges, no more incentive to suddenly raise the tariffs just to piss off a competitor or an enemy. One thing remained urgent, the preservation of our natural resources and therefore the protection of any organic and migratory activities.

The newly elected head of the Earthican Council included visits to Sanctuaries around the world as a diplomatic act to somehow advertise the fact that she was not only an atheist but she was also a follower of the Waral way of life. During her first campaign, Anita did put her heritage and background on the front lines, she was also able to charm some of her most conservative critics. As religious views have taken a step back for political and legislative life, the subject is still relevant. Almost every head of state as well as former heads of the Earthican Council have always used their religious views in order to enforce certain policies or to simply amass as much funds as possible. Anita was different in that she never used her absence of faith to enforce her political agenda; the questions came flocking by themselves. The fact that she was following a path that was still quite new at the time, was not made public until the media and journalists eventually figured it out. As a result, the newly elected Head of the Earthican Council was persuaded to push the Waral way of life onto the public stage. Anita was lucky enough to find regular, traditional as well as eccentric followers of the Way of life willing to shine under the light of public intricacy, if not just for a brief moment. The newly elected head of the Earthican Council visited many Sanctuaries, all of which were even more eccentric than the last. At the Sanctuary of the Chocolatine, in Northern new Gaul, Anita and her entourage managed to get an interview with Sister Odéna.

Odéna was a special kind of Waral instructor; she was the best theological teacher. Sister Odéna had moved to the North East of New Gaul from central Africa long before the year Alpha. In what was once called the kingdom of Belgium, Odéna joined a clerical order, became a bride of Keressus and worked in an orphanage for years. During her formative years as a nun, she was able to raise many children in need. She later lost the desire to follow any deity and when the kingdom finally fell, Odéna discovered her true passion: science and history. Odéna soon started to follow the path of the Waral way of life and became an Instructor at the Sanctuary of the Chocolatine. This innocent chat proved to the world that even if the Warals do not follow any deity, they still have a deep theological knowledge and understanding. Odéna was asked about her family and her siblings living in the Greater United States of America. Odéna was enchanted to answer all these personal and intimate questions. Sister Odéna had been living as a nun for so many years that everybody still called her Sister out of respect. Sister Odéna was delighted to tell the cameras about her former relationship with God. She also talked about her eternal relationship with her adopted son Noël. Sister Odéna was happy to receive attention. She knew the political nature of this interview, but she did not mind. On the contrary, this interview was a formidable opportunity to show off the productive life happening here, in the Sanctuary of la Chocolatine at the top of the Alps.

On every little home screen, the head of the Earthican Council could be seen chatting with a former nun. This was an attempt to court the conservatives. During another voyage, the head of the Earthican Council visited her birth town in Senegal and toured the rest of the continent. Up in the rocky hills of the horn of Africa, she visited a Sanctuary where she interviewed another Instructor, Professor Armel Hernandez, a former micro genetic biologist and his husband Makel Rapilnoski. Armel, originally from Bolivia, met his companion Makel, an extremely talented Ukrainian born engineer at the University of Barcelona. After graduation they started a strictly urban life together, both eventually became teachers, got married and finally decided to move away from Europe to retire in a warmer climate in search for a friendly environment to pursue their respective projects. The couple had been living in the Sanctuary for about ten years and appeared to be ravished. This interview showcased the importance of science as well as tolerance among the followers of the Waral way of life. This was of course an attempt to court the liberals. When Anita travelled to North America she had the rare occasion of meeting with some of the most eccentric Waral characters, notably the hippies at the Naturist Sanctuary of the Phoenix in the South, were she met with a colony of Warals that as the name implied always lived in the nude. The head of the Earthican council also met with the Monitor of the third Blooming Sanctuary, an old man living alone in a "mono" Sanctuary buried deep in the Appalachian Mountains in the East. Anita also met with a group of Instructors at the Academic Sanctuary of Didoux, what appeared to be the nerdiest place on planet, located in the remote forest of Quebec. The newly elected head of the Earthican council and her original administration was quite popular during her term in office, she kept most if not all her promises. She revitalised the economy and appeased the violent minds by offering alternatives and pushing back on violent entertainment. Anita managed to push a viable series of environmental policies like the famous Enclosed Power Facilities and the now well known Deep Sea Generators. When the time came to seek a second term she refused. The one term seeker had accomplished her task, honoured her promise to serve only one term and it was time for her to move on. Her legacy can still be observed today. As for the wild routes, they are flourishing. Wildlife is able to migrate in peace across cities, states, countries and principalities. As for the natural coastal protection measures, the revitalisation of mangroves and swamps to acts as a buffers against natural disasters are doing their job pretty well. These natural measures don't cost much to maintain. Clerical groups and organisations as well as Regal families across the globe did not particularly enjoyed having a Waral as a the head of the Earthican council for a few years, but these same individuals were not completely displeased either. After all the nature of the Earthican government is to give enough liberties to individuals, their countries and their cultures. The international direct popular vote was an undeniable force, this was the pulse of the Earthican population. This pulse could no longer be interfered with. Even if some territories still operated like backward gang states the Earthican population itself was entirely responsible for the election of each head of the Earthican council. Anita kept a relatively neutral and yet effective approach towards governmental policies and legislatures. The technologies and weaponry advancements were in full expansion, but since the end of international conflicts, this particular industry had blown out of proportion due to private demands for protection. After the sordid shooting years leading to the year Alpha, weapon companies started to develop magnetic freezers to disengage traditional guns. That led to the creation of harpoon like tools to protect snare, advertised as baggers. Eventually the crime organisation developed heating weapons, called heaters these were not vulnerable to freezers nor baggers. The heating weapon technologies have been subjected to ethical debts, the fact that these weapons were practically mislabeled lasers, pushed the government to develop their own heating weaponries. It seems that crime, violence and the appetite for intimidation will never be suppressed from human nature. Even in the most peaceful, modern and responsible society there will always be a few with an appetite that measures only to the fiercest predators. It has to be noted that crime and violence is becoming more spectacular, yet numbers don't lie and prove that somehow the rate is going down.

## 24 A WARAL MUST HONOUR THE LAWS OF LAND UPON WHICH THIS WARAL STANDS AND ROAM.

Passage from "Letters to a fellow Waral enthusiast", written by Genari Lemerii in late 2062 AD. Translated by the second grey Scribe. Original manuscript kept at the Sanctuary of the Roquaille, Scandinavia. (First distributed in the year Alpha zero point two)

Karim Bimpe, the beautiful one, was a strong and ferocious man, but he was also one of the kindest individuals that has ever walked the lands.Last year I had the pleasure to receive an invitation from the Scribe belonging to a Sanctuary. The Sanctuary was buried deep in the traitorous mountains in central Africa. Upon my arrival I was greeted by an old man accompanied by two of his most loyal friends. The old man had a walking stick and he loved to point things and people with it more than he needed to walk. This old man's name was Mkumbe, he was the personal assistant and attache of the Monitor of this remote Sanctuary. Mkumbe liked to greet visitors himself, but he was never alone. By his side was a bald giant and a small man with a terrifying history. The giant's name was Kemehjo but he was given the nickname Petit Jean because of his imposing stature. Petit Jean, or Little John, had a gift. It was not his mechanical and engineering prowesses that made him a sort of super star in the region. It was his exceptional linguistic talents. Petit Jean was born in one of the poorest cities in the land. To make ends meet, he started to repair all the machines and vehicles presented to him. Sometimes he would just work for free, just to help new faces in distress. One morning he was presented with a tiny device that he had never seen before; it was a small magnetic tool. Petit Jean was informed by the owner of the contraption that it had the power to disable fire arms. Petit Jean was absolutely baffled by this piece of equipment. This was a Freezer, a very popular disabling tool. Petit Jean had never worked nor repaired a Freezer before but he knew what to do; one of the secondary coils needed to be repaired. Because of his enormous hand he was not able to fix the device himself so he instructed his assistants. Because of his gigantic brain, Petit Jean managed to drive his assistants in the most precise manner. The owner of the Freezer stood there, observing the giant speaking to his assistants in one language, speaking the phone in another language and studied the inscriptions written on the Freezer that were yet in another language. Petit Jean was able to replace the damaged coil with the help of his trusted assistants without even laying a hand on the device. The owner of the device thanked Petit Jean and paid him and his assistants generously. The old man with the cane placed the Freezer back in his pocket and inquired;

" You! The gifted giant. How many languages do you speak?"

"About a dozen languages and two dozen patois" answered Petit Jean.

"I need a man of your talents" said the old man. " I want you to be my personal translator. I want you to work with me. My work implies that I travel the continent in search of new talented individuals such as yourself. Traveling across the land of Ferika means that I have to respect and honour the laws of each nation that I enter. After all, a Waral must honour the laws of the land upon which this Waral stands and roam. You will travel with me and act as my personal interpreter. You will make good money. Will you accept the job?"

Petit Jean looked a bit confused. He was not expecting such an offer and he was concerned about his repair shop.

"I would love to be an interpreter and travel the land of Ferika" admitted Petit Jean. "But I cannot leave my shop. I refuse to fire my assistants. Many families depend on the success of this shop. I can't quit. I won't quit."

"Who said anything about quitting?", said the old man. " If you work with me I'll take good care of your shop and your employees. All you have to do is to find a way to delegate and train your assistants. One of your assistants can manage your business during your absence. If you work with me, you will make more money. I guarantee that. And you will be able to travel and put your linguistic talents to good use."

And this is how the old man persuaded the giant to work with him. As for Karim Bempe, it is an entirely different story.

One morning, the old man and the giant were informed of the sudden death of Saint Bernard, a notorious local warlord. After terrorising the area with a firm hand for over twenty years, the rule of Saint Bernard was finally over. The same day a group of teenagers approached the old man's remote Waral Sanctuary. The boys looked sickly and emaciated. They looked like walking skeletons. They had escaped Saint Bernard's camp a few days before. One of the teenagers died the same evening and an other the next morning. Only two of the boys remained and they were dancing dangerously with death. Only one survived. This young man was small and was baring scars all across his face, his shoulders and his arms. The remote Waral Sanctuary nursed the young man back to health. The old man introduced himself;

"I am Mkabe, welcome. We are glad that you are healthy now, what is your name? Where do come from?"

" I am Karim Bempe, I am from Nigeria originally." Said the young man.

" Hello Bempe, do you know where you are?" asked the giant.

" Yes," said the young man," this is a Waral Sanctuary, the home of Ferika; one of the most secretive Waral Sanctuaries in the world".

" Yes, yes it is. How do you know about all that?" inquired the old man.

"I know everything there is to know about the Warals. I even know about the Book of Poisons" replied Karim.

"The Book of Poisons is a very dangerous tool," said the old man. " There is only one copy and nobody really knows where it is. Few Warals had the pleasure, or displeasure of reading such a document."

Karim Bempe spoke very little but his words were honest and true;

" My ancestors helped create the Book of Poisons. I am a hatchling and now that Saint Bernard is dead I am free. Free to learn how to follow the Waral way of life".

Karim was the second youngest of a family of healers from northern Nigeria. He grew up around wild beasts, rare herbs and extraordinary doctors. His father was a hyena man, a dancer and an entertainer. His mother was a leaf doctor, she was able to cure almost any disease known to man. His older brother was a snake handler and venom extractor, his task was to make medicine. His uncle was an ape and monkey expert, a local tourist guide and a poacher hunter. When Karim was very young he was kidnapped by Saint Bernard and was forced to become a child soldier. By the age of six, Karim was already able to carry an automatic rifle. By the age of eight he was addicted to brown brown. Saint Bernard used brown-brown to control his sanguinary troops. The potent drug made of cocaine, gun powder, leonotis pollen and datura fruits was a way to insure that the soldiers would become fearless and completely reliant on Saint Bernard's distribution of the drug. Karim tried to escape the clutches of Saint Bernard more than once. When Saint Bernard and his goons died, Karim was finally able to escape. It did not take long for Mkambe and Petit Jean to figure out that the demise of the warlord and his gang had been orchestrated by Karim himself. Karim Bempe, the beautiful one, may have been broken physically and morally. But he was smart and strong and he was determined to put an end to the rule of the warlord. The young man was ready to sacrifice his life for the better good. As a last resort, Karim poisoned the entire stash of brown brown, therefore killing all the users including Saint Bernard himself. The young man was compelled to take a dose of the lethal drug to avoid suspicion. Miraculously, Karim and three other boys did not immediately succumb to the effect of the deadly drug. A Waral legend persists today, it tells that the offspring of the authors of the book of poisons know the book of poisons even without reading it. They have an intact genetic memory of the book. I have trouble believing in such a silly story, but I must admit that meeting Karim in person led me to question many assumptions. When I met Karim, he was in his mid twenties. He had been working closely with the Waral Sanctuary. He was also involved with poacher prevention programs. The purpose of my voyage was to meet the Scribe of this Sanctuary. After a brief interview with the Monitor and the Scribe , the old man and the giant left me in the capable hands of Karim. The young man was to help me reach my next destination. Karim knew about my passion for the history of the Warals. I will always remember what he said to me when we finally parted ways;

"You must understand that I am not supposed to be alive. I should have died with the other soldiers years ago. The Waral Sanctuary taught me how to be myself. I have learned to forgive all the atrocities that I have committed. I have finally learned to forgive myself."

"What are you talking about?" I asked" You killed Saint Bernard and his gang. You are a hero. Your actions have prevented the death of countless innocents".

"Nobody is innocent," said Karim." We are all humans, we are all the same. We are all connected.

Desperate behaviours are the result of desperate individuals. If bad apples can climb the military ladder and the political ladder it is because people let them. No body is innocent. Everybody is responsible. We must honour the laws of nature as well as the laws created by man. We must love our fellow man. We have to fight for what we love, not against what we hate. There is a lot of hate inside of me but it is unequal to the love I carry with me were ever I go. There I leave you to your next travels, you must remember our little discussion. Always respect the laws upon which you stand and never forget about our connection with the laws of nature. You are welcome to come back, the doors of the Waral Sanctuary of Akgo are not easy to find, but they are always open."

## 25 WARALS DO NOT SEEK FAME NOR FORTUNE, THEY SEEK WISDOM.

Passage from the journal of the Monitor of the Sanctuary of the Southern plains, Southern Africa. Entry dating from summer 1879 AD. Manuscript translated and owned by Remji Bgou from the Lesser Oceanian Museum, Oceania. (Published in the year Alpha zero point two)

Every once in a while an individual is raised under the protection and the guidance of a lucky star. These lucky stars can take the form of relatives, guardians or friends. One of these individuals under the protection of a lucky star is known to the Warals as the third Purple scribe. The story of the third Purple scribe starts in the European Northern lands. The Warals archives tell that the Purple scribe was born in a palace in a city of lights. It is said that the Purple scribe had renounced any royal claims. This individual had tried to break free from capricious royals and their imaginary gods. In other words, the third Purple scribe had to break free from the imperial family. The Purple scribe, being of royal blood, had received a strict military training by the Dragoon elite. Years later, after obtaining a military position outside of Europe, the Purple scribe staged one of the most dramatic and theatrical ambushes in history. We know exactly what happened thanks to the private journal of the Monitor of the Sanctuary of Lenidu.

" Journal of the Monitor of the Sanctuary of Lenidu, summer 1879 AD. Today we heard of an attack a few kilometres from our Sanctuary. This was another attack perpetrated by the English. They are not respecting the rules of war, not even among themselves. Today a white man came to our Sanctuary. He looked like an English officer but he did not sound like an Englishman. He said that he was the sole survivor of an ambush, he was in desperate need of a meal and a place to hide for the night. He promised to leave at first light the next day. We happily agreed to let him stay for the night and we offered him fruits and vegetables. He only took the red fruits and went straight to bed. The next morning only his clothing remained. None of us saw him leave the Sanctuary. Two days later the white man returned. He was wearing a warrior's cloak, generously given to him by a Zulu prince the day before. The man insisted on seeing me alone. He wanted to make up for his strange behaviour. The man had convinced some of his friends, close relatives of the Zulu prince, to stage a fake ambush. The plan was to drive a small English battalion away while the man would stay behind consequently appearing to be killed by the Zulu attackers. The plan was executed with care. The Zulu warriors scared the battalion away, the man fell off his horse and like a skilful actor engaged into battle. The man howled as loud as he could and used his pistol twice. He fired one shot in the air and a second shot directly pointed at the ground. The man made sure that his battalion heard his screams and the two shots fired. He had to make sure that the English fleeing in the distance saw him engage into a fight to the death with the Zulu warriors. Once the English were out of sight, the man thanked his friends for staging the attack and they laughed. Then he told the warriors that they were no longer needed and sent his regards to the Zulu prince. Next step of his plan was to find a place to hide for the night, a place close enough to the fake battlefield. This is how the man found our Sanctuary. The man left his clothing behind and walked back to the site where the fake ambush had taken place. The man carefully smeared juice from the red fruit all over one side of his body. He kept the flesh of the red fruit and placed it on one of his eyes. Then the man laid on the floor next to a broken spear and a shield left behind by one of the mighty warriors. There he remained naked and lifeless the entire day until an English unit returned to the battle field. The unit confirmed the identity of the carcass laying on the ground and after a brief discussion with the Zulu warriors it was concluded that the man had started the fight and had paid the price with his life. The man was declared dead. His body was then strategically switched up with another casualty of war that resembled him. The remains were sent back to Europe. After staging his own death, the white man asked to stay in our Sanctuary. He told me that he felt the need to change his destiny. The white man was tired of the European ways, he wanted to discover the world, the real world. He wanted to study with our Instructors. He was eager to learn how to follow the Waral way of life, in his mind that was the right path for him. The man who would one day be known as the Purple scribe had embrace the natural and mechanical world, his life was no longer dictated by royalty. He came to realise that deities had absolutely no power over his life. His own Warality was his own power, the new essence of his existence. As a Monitor I had to determine his goals, his desires as well as his ambitions. I informed him that the Warals do not seek fortune or glory, they seek Warality; the ultimate wisdom. When I inquired about his future and his new role in the world the young man bluntly replied;

" I was born as the richest child of an imperial family and yet money has rendered me miserable. Every notable, every clergyman, every parent and every child in the land knew who I was, but I was not able to meet them. The fortune and the fame to which I have inherited should have made me a happy man. Quite the contrary, every day and every night I dream about remoteness and anonymity. For this reason I have planned my death in order to pursue my own life. I see a path driver by wisdom for myself. I want to learn how to live with less. I want to study the arts of science without having to answer to a priest. I have no desire to ascend to heaven or to dive in hell, I want to make use of my natural abilities. I want to be a part of our world, not try to dominate it like I was raised to do."

## 26 ONE OF A WARAL'S MANY ROLES IS TO PRESERVE AND PROTECT HUMANITY'S NATURAL AND CULTURAL HERITAGE.

Veragas speech at the annual meeting of the Earthican Waral Association. Speech recorded in Benjamin Dreyfus journal and translated by the Scribe of the dunes. Journal on display at the Sanctuary of the dunes, EurAsia. (Distributed early in the year Alpha zero point four)

"My friends, we are all gathered here today to celebrate the creation of our wonderful association ten years ago. Look what we have accomplished together. This year we have with us representatives and attachés of Waral

Sanctuaries from over a hundred nations. Together, in partnership with our nation's government as well as the assistance of the Earthican council we have obtained the respect, the protection and the exposure that our way of life deserves. Each year new Sanctuaries with new ideas are built all over the world. Each and every one of these new Sanctuaries is cementing new traditions and new techniques. Each of these Sanctuaries are forming new scribes. Each one of these scribes has the potential to continue the Waral code and its peaceful intentions. Ladies, gentlemen and others, we have a long meeting ahead of us and I know how far you have travelled. As we all know; one of a Waral's many roles is to preserve and protect humanity's natural and cultural heritage. Let us share memories, all gathered around this feast. Speaking of which, I am not the only hungry person in the room so without further ado, allow me to read you the menu of today;

Traditional Moroccan vegetable couscous Tajine, accompanied by chicken or fish.

Parisian Parmentier made from red potatoes with sweet potato cakes.

Traditional European Bûche Log with frozen ice-creamed cake.

Traditional Thai Pla dish, containing steamed fish of your choice with steam vegetables and rice swimming in secret lemon sauce.

Haitian veggie combo with local Pikliz, a traditional sweet slaw, accompanied by Makawoni Aw Graten.

Walkabout banquet contains all possible and imaginable meals to be shared during the same occasion.

There are so many beautiful things on this buffet that I will not bore you and enumerate each delicacy. But I want to remind you all that we all have the possibility to opt for a vegetarian version of each dish.

Bon appétit mes amis.

## 27 THE WARALS ACKNOWLEDGE THAT CONFLICT IS SOMETIMES INEVITABLE, BUT VIOLENCE MUST NEVER BE USED AS A RESOLUTION FOR SAID CONFLICTS.

Second chapter of "Rising against the rule of the Dragoons; a manual of self defence". Antique book dating from 1619 AD, copied and owned by the third blue Scribe of the Mono Sanctuary #427, Germania. (Published in the year Alpha zero point four)

As the Chelonian forces relinquished the possibility of raging war against the rule of the Dragoons, an old Monitor from a nearby Sanctuary was asked for Council. The Draggoons had mounted troops ready to attack the walls of the serpentine city, the army of Chelone had no choice but to be absolutely prepared. The Monitor was asked for help, the Chelonian Council needed to find a way to better the assailant. The Monitor, by definition a former Instructor herself, had no interest in violence but the Chelonians pressed on and were desperate.

"You are the Waral we have been looking for" said the head of the Chelonian Council.

"How do you know?" replied the Monitor.

The head of the Chelonian Council stood up and asked with a fervent voice; "You are the old woman who taught our ancestor how to tame the mightiest war elephants are you not? You are the one who showed us how to use the speed and the strength of the fiercest predators to our advantage are you not? You are the one who saved the life of my mother with your herbs are you not?"

"Yes, I am". Replied the Monitor.

"If you want to preserve the existence of your precious Sanctuary and your precious lands, you have to tell the inhabitants of the city of Chelone how to defend the Dragoons once and for all."

"That I cannot do" admitted the old woman "for you see a Waral without compassion is no Waral at all. A Waral doesn't believe in violence. I must add to this statement that Warals do acknowledge that conflict is sometimes inevitable, but violence must never be used as a resolution for said conflict."

"You Warals are such a band of hypocrites," said one of Council members." You call yourselves a spiritual community yet most of you claim that you are not a religious order. You teach us how to develop new methods to kill our enemies yet you say you are against violence, you claim to be on the side of peace and justice yet you always avoid being stained by the touch of a neighbour in need."

"With all due respect" said the Monitor, " that couldn't be further from the truth. The Warals have been turned between conflicts for thousands and thousands of years. Every war, every army, every enemy has sought the wisdom of the followers of the Waral way of life at one point or another. I regret to inform you that we can no longer be part of your genocidal campaigns. We do not answer to your gods, nor we can deny their influence that they have over your lives and your dubious desires. With the same intense feeling, we do not answer to crowned individuals. Their royalty or their imperial moods do not impress us. The Dragoons had tried to get rid of the Warals for generations, but still we are a part of the same world. The followers of the Waral way of life have yet to concede and disappear. Out there, beyond these walls, a horde of highly trained mounted Dragoons is about to raid and pillage your ancestral home. Tis not a follower of the Waral way of life to rescue overtime an obstacle presents itself to you. I had the same conversation with the Emperor Sfanern two days ago and I am going to tell you what I told him then..."

"You spoke with our sworn enemy two days ago?" interrupted the head of the council.

"I did." Answered the old woman calmly, then she continued her speech: " The world created by the rule of the Dragoons and the world developed by Chelone are one and the same for the followers of the Waral way of life are forced to live between the two worlds that you have created, we can but be spectators of your own demise. Our Sanctuaries are sacred environments and for some of us these Sanctuaries are regarded as places of worship. Places where each Waral is able to worship love, compassion, science, world history without prejudice, good taste, agronomics, arts and other delicate activities that are regarded both by the Chelonians and the Dragoons as frivolous activities. Ladies, gentlemen and other members of the council of Chelone, I regret to inform you that I have only one advice for you all if you wish to put an end to this assault before it even takes place; the head of the Council of Chelone must have a meeting with the emperor of the Dragoons in order to discuss terms of disarmament."

The entire council was shocked and appealed to the senior members to refuse such an inappropriate suggestion. But the Monitor did not flinch:

" Chelone is in search of more land. The Dragoons care about resources. The Chelonian population is growing at a remarkable paste and so does the extent of the rule of the Dragoons. Both your worlds have been raging war against each other but you have the same exact dream. Both your worlds are looking forward to peace and prosperity. The followers of the Waral way of life only desire privacy, so please keep us out of your conflicts. As a matter of fact I advise you to treat and trade with the Dragoons. Any emperor can be purchased for the right price, the same goes for any of heads of the Chelonian council past and present company included. Your deities are in conflicts with the divine regality imposed by the Dragoons. Stop at once. Preserve human lives, this massacre has to stop. When the Dragoons and the everlasting city of Chelone will see eye to eye, both parties will see a substantial increase of profits and land expansion."

"Are you trying to imply that we unify with the Dragoons?" asked one of the members.

"No, you are not ready for that yet" said the Monitor," I simply imply that if both your worlds want to survive you have to misplace this animosity between you peoples, I strongly suggest that you put an end to the violence to make place for an era of mentally and financially rewarding rivalry. This driven by competition and the desire to trade goods and services that you wouldn't normally get exposed to can resolute, or at least ease the tensions between your two interconnected worlds. Chelone, the eternal serpentine city and the appetite of the Dragoon regality, working side by side and perhaps together once in a while, could be a much more profitable experience than war."

"And the emperor Sfanern agrees with you?" asked the head of the council.

"Only if you are" said the old woman" The followers of the Waral way of life, the population of the mighty Chelonian City and the orders of the Dragoons have to agree to put an end to the violence together, or else peace will not be achievable. Chelone needs to lay down her arms, the Dragoons need to stop their attacks and the Warals can no longer teach about the taming and healing methods from the book of poisons. The world that you have created have been amassing enough blood and nourishment from slavery, genocide, displacement, mistrust and complete disrespect for one another. The conflicts between your worlds are not without tribulations but you must stop the violence at once if you do not want to perish. This is the only way to save your respective citizens and subjects. If you and the Dragoons want to save your profits and your divine ways we must all agree to a truce, all of us. The Dragoons, Chelone and the followers of the way of life, all of us must learn to agree to disagree in order to solve our differences."

The same day a meeting was arranged. The council of Chelone, Sfanren and his Dragoons and the Elders of the nearby Sanctuary signed a truce, cease fire was ordered promptly and the Monitor was allowed to return to Sanctuary. This is only one of many truces and cease fires arranged by the Warals in the hope to unify the world of Chelone and the world ruled by the regalia Dragoons. Many legends told by the Warals insinuates that a true peace between the two worlds will only be achieved when both parties will see an external element on the verge of threatening their continuations. Indeed a Waral tale has survived to this day. It is a tale that describes a world, not so distant from ours, that will inevitably force the eternal serpentine city of Chelone and the land ruled by Dragoons to work, live and survive together against threatening forces standing at the gates of the skies, surrounding the land of Ferika and all the lands of the globe. In this tale, the Warals are an insignificant group on the edge of society; forgotten by the descendants of Chelone and the descendants of the lands ruled by the Draggons. The tale of the external forces has been told once or twice, but never thrice.

## 28 TOTEMS AND SIGNS ARE ONLY ARTEFACTS TO HELP A WARAL FOCUS. THEY ARE THE BASIS FOR A WELL CONDUCTED RITUAL, BUT THEY ARE NOT NECESSARY.

Accounts noted by an I.T. analyst dating from 1999 AD. Digital information retrieved, decoded and translated by the restless Scribe. Original computer hardware kept at the Sanctuary of Robotics, Switzerland. (First distributed in the year Alpha zero point nine)

Cedric Jaden, I.T. consultant, report of the hard drive #E-345617-2 sent by Instructor Mauricette from the Sanctuary of Robotics.

File 1 Witch and famous; relationship between totems and rituals.

Document Z-61025 message decoded by unit 613: "Maybe you're a Druid, maybe you're a Mage. Maybe you're a Sage, a Sorcerer and found of letters. They love you when you're optimistic man. They hate you when you're realistic man. Cast a spell on me you're witch and famous, nobody's to blame, hold on to that flame. Maybe you're Cool, maybe you're Old school. Maybe you're a fool, maybe I'm a Toad. Floating in a cup, flying like a Snake. Extinguished and washed out by the Rain." After a diligent analysis our team has been able to conduct a thorough research. The goal of our research was to determine if the community known as "the followers of the Waral way of life" are in fact making use of items and ceremonial activities. As surprising as it may, our results have determined with certitude that individuals following this way of life belong to a few distinct groups. All of them agree on the core factors of their hardest beliefs, however is should be noted that some followers of the Warals way of life rely on certain artefacts ( figurines, music instruments, chants, literature, discussions, candles, essence and other traditional hand crafted objects) others prefer to rely solely on organic materials considered sacred by some and essential by others ( geological fragments, animal pelts, bones, skins, feathers, an assortment of sage, tobacco, cannabis, vanilla, thyme and other herbs). Not all of these individuals are making use of these articles. Most acknowledge that these articles are the basis for a well conducted ritual, but they are not necessary. The articles and items are known as material-totems or objects to facilitate the conduct of ritualistic ceremonies. Our research points to a certain conclusion that some Warals have a deep relationship with these objects, it is a way to materialise their thoughts. Totems and signs are only artefacts to help a Waral focus. They are the basis for a well conducted ritual, but they are not necessaryThe use of these object and other materials are considered, by some, an essential part of any ritual. The rituals of the individuals known as " the followers of the Waral way of life" are known as celebrations. These can be compared to traditional weddings, funerals, wakes and rites of passage. Our research concludes that Warals are a non violent and educated community. Every individual following the path of the Waral way of life is intimately and sentimentally attached to the Waral code, a set of guidelines revolving around acceptance and education. Therefore it is inconceivable that any authority should prevent these individuals from building a better future for themselves.

File 2 Data from the Mechanical Forces headquarters announcing take over of every station above 2000 feet, reference and memos about the importance of signs.

Document Z-81203 reply decoded by unit 613: " Mechanical Forces riposte, casualties above. Mechanix dangerous driving force. Earthican accords signed by Mechanix, but refused by Natural Front. Council in limbo, Mechanical Forces claimed D2 station, C3 station as well as all remaining objects one hundred feet above the tallest facility on Earth. Speaker for the Mechanical Forces has claimed ceasefire against Earthican citizens but has declared the Natural Front as an enemy of the Forces." Our nano technicians have retrieved a series of messages transmitted by the official representative of the Mechanical Forces provisional government. All of these communications have been addressed to the Earthican council. None of these communications implicate any assistance from the individuals known as " the followers of the Waral way of life". However one message implies that a member of the Mechanical Forces have been in irregular contact with the leaders of the Natural Forces in order to address a resolution to their conflict. Our nano technicians do not have the means to pursue and conduct their research to the standards of our Agency. We have contacted a resident of the Sanctuary of Robotics and asked her to share any information regarding these doubtful communications. Our report is simple: the resident of the Sanctuary of robotics has suggested that the Mechanix and the Natural Front are having crossed communications. It has been suggested that the Natural Front is making use of sophisticated means of communication to deliver messages in orbit and the Mechanics are sending undetectable organic messages down on the surface. This conclusion makes absolute sense to my colleagues and myself. The Mechanical Forces are no longer an orbital militia, they have organised themselves and their technological progress should not be negligible. Our research has proven that the provisional government of the Mechanical Forces are desperate to reach an organic agreement in order to pursue their orbital agriculture and expansion. We must insist that the Earthican council makes a decisive move to prevent this orbital from taking over the surface. We advise that the Mechanical Forces be stopped by all means necessary.

File 3 Collection of pictures and personal files about diverse residents of the Sanctuary of Robotics, again another reference/memo relating the importance of totems, spirit animals, signs, etc.

Document Z-90123 message decoded unit 613: " I am calling you and all your loved ones to rise above hate and prejudice. Express your deepest sympathies, engorge the power of love. Those who chose to remain nude and silent should be able to do so. Those who desire to chant, dance and perform ritualistic meditations should be able to do so. Totems and signs are only artifices to help a Waral focus. They are the basis for a well conducted ritual, but they are not necessary. Look into your heart, what does it tell you? Is it telling you to roar like the Lion? How about your vision? Is it as precise and persevering like the Falcon? Or perhaps you have attained the vigorous wisdom of the Serpent? Is it possible that all these animal totems mean nothing to you? Perhaps all animal totems mean something to you. I am calling you and your loved ones to rise above magic and superstition. I invite you to feel and express your attachment or non attachment to your signs, plant and animal totems as well as material artefacts. For those who follow the path of the Waral way of life must understand that our philosophy isn't dogmatic nor totalitarian, each of us has the duty to answer to our most precious natural law. One law; one love." After a long discussion with the resident of the Sanctuary of Robotics it is easy to detect that the followers of the Waral way of life have an extraordinary loose organisation revolving around one single law. This law includes all Warals to respect the choices of individuals. One law; one love, encompasses a series of ethical and moral agreements that are all oriented towards non violence and education. Our research has proven that no two Waral are the same and that no two Warals practice this discrete philosophy the same way. Some individuals are emotionally attached to their objects, rituals, celebrations and artefacts. Others are not so committed and just observe a sporadic celebration here and there. When the Mechanical Forces first contacted the Sanctuary of Robotics, the Monitor of the establishment relayed the information to the Earthican council. The local authorities were able to conduct their research and recognition operation with complete cooperation from the part of the Sanctuary. Our conclusion is that the Warals are strictly opposed to conflicts. It would be foolish to refuse a partnership with these individuals known as " the followers of the Waral way of life".

## 29 TOTEMS AND SIGNS DO NOT POSSESS ANY POWERS, THEY ARE ONLY SELF-MOTIVATIONAL TOOLS.

Communication and rituals; second page from the program of the minutes from the meeting of The Healers, recorded by Inspector S.D.Q. in 2046 AD. Partial manuscript translated and owned by the Pepper Scribe of the Sanctuary of Limino, Central America. (Published on Claudiary the 14th of the year Alpha two point fourteen)

Third annual meeting of the healers and inspectors, autumn 2046 AD. Presence is non mandatory but dully encouraged; meeting starts at noon and will end once all important matters are resolved. Attendance respected by all healers of the lands including the seven Inspectors,the twelve Scribes, all known Orators and all Monitors of the highlands (apart from the Monitor of the Lone Valley). Minutes recorded by Sabrina D. Quince.

Affairs of the day: conversations between healers to compare notes about the importance, or irrelevance of totems, signs and ritualistic methods applied to summons, events or personal enlightenment.

The objective is to determine why totems and signs do not possess any powers and why they are nearely self motivational tools.

List of totems, objects and significant methods presented on this day:

Wind chants presented by Max Habyl the Hoo Hi Han Orator of Hakai.

Fire and Earth rhythms performed by the Monitor of the Great terrain of San.

Air demonstration presented by Mekouméle, the Scribe of the Ghanii Bands.

Sacred objet d'Art exposed by Xi Du, the Orator of Nkemet.

Hstu (bull roars) and Pstu (didgeridoos) carving demonstration supervised by Donnie Paulton the Inspector of the Northern Oceanic basin.

Grass blade and other natural communication techniques presented by Riding Blade, the Orator of Clementville .

## 30 A WARAL MUST SHARE THE HISTORY OF THE WARAL WAY OF LIFE.

Passage from "The Twelve Predicators". Partial book with missing pages, allegedly written by the first Bright Scribe, date unknown. (Published in eastern Europe in the year Alpha three point one)

The twelve Predicators and their visions:

The twelve Predicators are popular figures amongst the followers of the Waral way of life. They are regarded by most historical scholars as folk heroes, visionaries and healers. All of them believed that a true Waral must share the history of the Waral way of life. Sharing their heritage and their precious folk tales was the only way to preserve their culture and a perfect method to protect their own future. There was Ferika who had a vision of a united humanity. The siblings Assam and Attam who saw a better future for themselves beyond the known lands. The Grey, bearer of messages of peace. A'Nena the communicator, who had a vision of a never ending communication spree. Xiu Ji, the one who was able to predict the return of the Dragoons. Veritix who tried to warn his tribe of the imminent attacks from the armies of the South. Bahadi Ka, the great protector and predicator of the demise of her lands. Radix who warned his masters against the plots perpetrated by the court. Quoqledo who led his troops away from carnage after having a vision of an invasion perpetrated by an unstoppable force. The leaf doctor Erïeldür and the leaf reader Eraëldur who, after seeing the future, united their respective villages and led them against the dictate of the Dragoons of the Northern plains. Door maker who, after having a vivid dream, realised that it was safer for his band to unite with the invaders and start a new life kilometres away from his native land. The one they call the Dark forces, who led a tumultuous Siberian life, tried to warn the world of Chelone and the Dragoons about a world conflict that would end the rule and the dictates of both civilisations.

Ferika, mother of modern man, born over two hundred thousand years ago, Predicator of the emergence of conflicts between Chelone, the rule of the Dragoons and the inevitable struggle of the followers of the Waral way of life. Her vision of a land shared by all. Ferika the teacher, the visionary, the educator. Her message was one of the first stories shared by the Warals. The name Ferika and the name of the land Ferika can be interpreted as two versions of the same myth.

Assam and Attam the traveling brothers, blood brothers and fervent practitioners of extensive Walkabouts were searching for new lands. The siblings parted ways over a hundred thousand years ago. As each of them was looking for a different type of landscape they promised each other to continue to share their ancestral ways across the distant plains, across the interminable river and across the skies. Their strategic and methodic personalities gave them the strength to persevere in their individual quests, all their methods and secrets have been passed on from generation to generation.

The one they call the Grey did not start to follow the path of the Waral way of life until middle age. No one knows if the Grey was a woman, a man or something else. Perhaps the Grey was so unique that all who listen to the messages delivered by the Grey became subjugated. Delivering a message of unity, the Grey was able to establish a strong presence in the far East until it was decided that the Grey would share a message of peace to all who would listen, from the rugged terrains of the West all the way down south towards the land of Ferika. Most Warals think the incredible journey of the Grey happened over fifty-thousand years ago. But no one knows for sure. To this day the life of the one they call the Grey remains a mystery, a beautiful mystery.

A'Nena the communicator had an extraordinary knowledge of the Red Island. His intricate work was simple; he wanted to learn to speak the language of nature. It is believed that A'Nena was born thirty-thousand years ago and that he lived two hundred years. He was a talented tracker and a great listener. In the morning he would build leaf shaped Hstus out of wood, he would attach them to a solid rope and twirl the mysterious objects in the air to call his family. After the first meal of the day he would look for dead branches hollowed by the termites. Once cleaned up and decorated he would make the branch sing and laugh by kissing one of the extremities of the branch and then he would teach everybody how to replicate his work. The list is quite long but believe me or not, these two incredible methods of communications are still used to this day.

Xiu Ji was a great warrior and protector of the central plateaux who patrolled the mighty trails almost ten thousand years ago. As she grew older she had a vision, a vision she had to hare with the rest of her family. She closed her eyes, took a deep breath and said: " Long after I am gone the Dragoons will return and try to take our land. One of you is going to have to learn the ways of war to prevent war. Long after I have rejoined the cycle of existence a great Khan will rise against the Dragoons, you duty is to await the arrival of your Khan. You will be given a choice, to fight and preserve your ways or abandon your ways and flee to the nearest Circle of Chelone or perhaps even worse; you may abandon your ways in favour of an offering made by the Dragoons. The choice is yours. You must share my vision and you must reach your final destination". Needless to say that her message was never forgotten.

Veritix was not a warrior nor a chief, in fact almost nobody remembers Veritix for the simple reason that his vision was flawed and forgotten by his own tribe. The event took place about three thousand years ago. Veritix was disgusted by the advancement of the Dragoons expanding their armies across the Gaulish lands. One day Veritix summoned the elders of his tribe and asked to speak to the chief in front of the elders. " Our tribe will die if we do not unite with our neighbouring tribes" he exclaimed. Everybody laughed. " If we do not unite immediately our way of life will be suppressed by the Dragoons" he continued. " We must make peace with our enemies, we must unite with them to form a greater tribe to scare the Dragoons away from our lands" he cried. Nobody listened, the chief killed Vertex on the spot for suggesting an alliance with other tribes. Half a century later his message was re-ignited by the son of one of the elders, this young man became chief and tried to put the teachings of Veritix into practice. But it was too late.

Bahadi Ka was a young mother when the Dragoons invaded her refreshing green island. She was forced to flee and hid for a time in the northern parts of her dear green Island. The Dragoons established their territory of Britania and the circle of Chelone grew thiner and thiner. The surviving followers of the Waral way of life had tried to warn the population of the green island but their message was ignored. They say that Bahadi's daughter was the one who led a resisting force against the fierce Dragoons, she had a vision of a green population united under one banner, one symbol. She continued to say that her ultimate goal was to live free. Bahadi tried to dissuade her daughter to go to war, she would not listen as she knew in her heart that freedom was better to be obtained than to serve as a slave for the Dragoons courts.

# IV Admixture:

The following spring a new threat emerged. The bloody plant had resurfaced with a vengeance. It was a stronger and hardier variety and it was about to terrorise the globe once more. Our first intervention of the year took us to South America. In the heart of Sao Paulo, one of the most populated and cosmopolitan cities on Earth where the plant was raging havoc. The shear size of the infested zone was too much for our agency to contain. Like governor Mare predicted the year before, a new agency was about to cast a shadow on our enterprise. And a very large shadow indeed. Multiple bio-control agencies were already on site. Our agency was the last one to arrive in Sao Paulo. We landed our Delivery Station on a makeshift landing platform. We all noticed our competitors unloading their armada, they were stationed all over the place. They appeared to be ready to greet us. As our drone touched the ground Babs, who was sitting next to me, shared her first impressions. She closely watched the competition's equipment through the window and said:

"Oh, dear, looks like they have a lot more toys than we do, and bigger ones too."

"This game is not about the toys", said Les. "It is about the players, and we are the best players."

During this intervention general Les Roken, my general Les Roken, managed to show off his commanding abilities. In an instant, he firmly established a security perimeter with the help of our security team. The perimeter was set around the infected area with the assistance from the other bio-control agencies. General Roken had this ability to coordinate with others and delegate tasks with the most surprising ease. Spending thirty years commanding the best army in the world probably thought him a thing or two. Our agency and our competitors managed to take control of the situation relatively fast. We were able to complete a precise eradication of the toxic plant. We also managed to collect enough samples of the new variety of this invading species for later analysis. The operation was finally over, it only took a couple of hours to neutralise our target. We could not have acted that fast without the help of the other bio-control agencies and general Roken's commanding talents. It was time to pack the equipment and move on to the next mission. The new toxic plant was conquering new grounds each passing day, we had to act fast. We have to analyse and study this new variety promptly. This was a very similar plant next to the variety from the year before. But the devil is always hiding in the details, so we have to conduct meticulous research. As we did so Zed, Babs and Mehdi made a horrifying discovery. This new variety of plant was defusing a much more violent compound than the variety from the previous year. Without further expertise it was going to be very difficult to find a new and effective antidote. Babs suggested that we ask her brother Burlington for help. Burlington or "Baggy" was a pioneer in Psychotropic and toxic substances. He made a name for himself, as well as a considerable fortune, when he became the most successful business man of the THC industry. Since the end of international cannabis and psychotropic prohibition, Baggy has created a brand new pharmaceutical empire for himself. Unfortunately he has been gravitating towards more virulent products lately. Baggy's experience was particularly useful in order to develop a new antidote. Colonel Roken was not fond of working with Baggy the 'rich junky'. Les eventually did put his feelings aside when he actually got to work with Baggy. Roken remarked that his initial judgement may have been unfounded, Roken has adopted a more flexible approach regarding Baggy's notorious lifestyle. After all, Noël and Baggy used to be friends. As teenagers, they played in a band together but they parted ways soon after Baggy decided to fly off the handle and experiment with all sorts of drugs and debauchery. And now, Baggy was asked to join our agency as a special member. He was to be assigned to the secondary laboratory on the top floor of the Delivery Station. The Anti-Bioterrorism and Bio-threat Agency was hovering across the land towards the next infected location and the entire team was on board. A meeting was taking place in the conference room:

"Mes amis," Said Noël," Burlington is going to meet us at the next infected zone".

"Let's hope that he doesn't look completely trashed when he meets us" added Les," that is if he can manage to find us ".

"Are you kidding?" asked Noël. "Baggy's got so much smack and cactus in his system that it is only when he is coming down that he looks trashed! "

"I hope you're right buddy", said Les. "I mean, he is flying from the western Mongolian plateau. That is one hell of a long flight. He is going to have plenty of time to get trashed up there."

"My baby brother is always 'up there'" said Babs.

"Are you having a laugh?" I asked sarcastically. "If Baggy is going to work with us, he is going to have to get his mind together. He is going to need to get his shit straight".

"Oh, that's what the young brides said!" said Zed. The young woman had a flare to throw jokes in the air during the most awkward times.

We arrived at the next location just on the outskirts of Lima and here was Baggy waiting for us. He was tipping from side to side and appeared to be high as a kite, as usual. He was standing on the edge of the landing platform. El Presidente and his entourage were also here standing by Burlington's side. The Delivery Station landed and we finally got to work. Burlington jumped on his station set up in the secondary lab on board the Drone. His expertise was put to good use. We successfully developed a new antidote. We also managed to contain and secure the infected zone. The eradication of the new variety of the toxic plant was conducted by books. Most importantly, we achieved to administer the antidote to the infected population. This antidote was able to counter the narcotic and contraceptive effects of the toxic plant. The new antidote was sent to facilities all around the globe for mass production. Every Earthican citizen was to be protected against the devastating effects of the new devastative variety. A rumour was circulating at the time; the Natural Front was expanding its activities in central and south America. But this was a tiny rumour compared to the tales surrounding the Warals. Many news articles at the time suggested that the toxic plant had been developed and unleashed by the followers of the Waral way of life. The Warals appeared to be in cahoots with the Natural Front. This was probably due to the fact that the Natural Front has been burrowing some of the most iconic symbols of the Warals ever since its creation. These were only folktales opposed to the real threat to our modern world; the orbital attacks perpetrated by the Mechanics. Every once in a while, our little home screens and our little wrist screens showed gruesome footage of a new disaster inflicted by explosive devices send by the Mechanics. Every week some reporter was enumerating the lives taken by the Mechanics. From their safe tactical operation above our heads, the Mechanics were still waging war. Their methods of destruction were getting more sophisticated each year. The Natural Front on the other hand was making use of more savage methods to fill every Earthican citizen minds with dread and terror. The Natural Front had this habit of filming their hostages, making good promises and filing the release of their hostages. While the camera was still filming the hostage getting away from the incarceration site full of hope, one of the members of the Front would simply shoot an arrow directly in the back of the former hostage. These barbarians used their victims as target practice and one legend surrounding the Front was that they made arrows with the bones of their victims. As I mentioned above, the Earthican nations no longer wage war against each other. But the barbaric attacks fermented by the Natural Front and the fire-power released from the heavens by the Mechanics still make the head of the evening news. The Mechanics deadly projectiles have claimed so many souls that I barely notice the chaos around me anymore.

Despite everything our job is very repetitive. We encounter new species and new challenges in our line of work but overall we follow the exact same protocol. Notably; contact with the targeted bio-threat, creation of a security perimeter, contain and eradicate the target, collect a few samples for later analysis, pack the equipment and leave. But on this day, everything changed in a flash. We had just accomplished our mission. The operation near Lima was over. We had just finished eradicating the toxic plant and we were starting to pack the equipment. I was reconnecting the PH tester to the main computer on board of the Delivery Station. I distinctly remember something peculiar, something was very off indeed. I could hear the security team talking outside of the Drone, Zed was next to me helping me with the computer. Baggy and Les were upstairs arguing about something in the secondary laboratory. I can distinctly remember Baggy asking:

" Who is flying this darn drone thing anyway?"

" Ted The Auto Pilot", answered Les." or TTAP for short."

Meanwhile Babs and Mehdi were checking the inventory and Noël was sitting behind his improvised desk in the open conference room. Mehdi's wrist screen was playing the famous song Wolf Totem. We all were ready to reach our next destination.

Then in an instant :(swish), pitch black! A hood was quickly placed upon my head. As I tried to wrestle in protest I felt a stunning sensation in the neck. Someone had infected me with a powerful tranquilliser. I was fainting rapidly but I could still decrypt the madness happening inside the Delivery Drone. And (zoom), we were transported quickly, or should I say nabbed. Next thing I knew I woke up in the middle of the jungle with my teammates. Noël, Zed, Babs, Les, Mehdi, Baggy and I were waking up, barely standing. We were surrounded by heavily armed individuals.

" Welcome to the rocky jungles of the Kongo Mountain chain" announced one of the men. He continued and informed us that he and his colleagues, had carried us about 3000 miles away from South America. As it turned out our initial kidnapers were outsmarted by the real individuals responsible for our travel across the Atlantic. One of the nabsters, a large and bold man, walked slowly towards Noël and announced:

"Bonjour mes amis. Hello Mister Clean, I apologise for the precautions. As you may have noticed my friends have been keeping an eye on for the past two years".

"No one," said Noël," no one has called me Mister Clean since..."

"Since the Nile monitor incident in Florida?", interrupted the big guy," yes, yes I know all about that. This is not important right now. What is important is that we have been observing your progress, from a safe distance. My friends and I were concerned about losing you to the Natural Front. These brutal thugs have been trying to catch you guys for a while. This afternoon they almost got their dirty hands on you, so we had to intervene and teach them some manners. We saw them injecting you with the drugs and we saw them putting the hoods on your heads. Since you and your security team were incapacitated we took the liberty of taking care of your aggressors. We brought you here while you were napping, you know, because of the drugs."

"T's all good dude" agreed Baggy." Those were pretty good drugs by the way".

My old friend Noël, with a defiant look in his eyes, faced the big guy and tried to protest:

"But I..."

"No butts my friend," said the big guy. "We have a long walk ahead of us. We brought you here for a reason. Someone very special wants to meet you. By the way, you and your friends must be hungry? What are your pleasures? I 'll tell the cook to prepare anything you desire".

"Well, since you have all the guns" admitted Noël," I guess we are going to oblige and order a little snack".

"Yes, please do. The chef is very talented." Replied the big guy. He informed us that our security team was still waiting for us in Lima on board the Delivery Drone, 3000 miles away from us.

We all did as we were told by the big bald guy. We ordered some of the most outrageous meals on purpose of course.

Babs requested tender veal escalopes with asparagus and a tiramisu for dessert. Without hesitation her brother asked for a double cheese burger with fries and a couple of chilled Coors light. Les ordered a large platter of steamed blue crabs with, and I quote; " tons of Old Bay and a bottle of white Bigfoot whine". I requested a Salade Niçoise, with a glass of Saint Maxime Rosé 58 and a Tarte à la Tropézienne for desert. Noël asked for a Thieboudienne and cider in French. Miss Turing ordered a whole chicken Basquaise, with red rice and an orange Fanta. Mehdi demanded an original vegetarian Moroccan Tajine, he also insisted on getting almond Briouats, his favourite pastries, for dessert.

"Okay my friends." Said the big guy "now I want you all to give me your phones, your wrist screens and your electronic devices please. We have electronic and magnetic freezers on stand by, you know these wonderful devices that can neutralise any weapon or electronic device? Well make sure you give it all away ".

We did as we were told and we all started to walk towards the mountains. I was still a bit confused and groggy due to the tranquilliser injected in my fecking neck a few hours earlier.

Babs. Les and Mehdi were helping me walking and keeping up with the group. This mountaineering caravan was composed of my friends and dear colleagues as well as our new heavily armed "friends". They were armed to the teeth. They had mechanical and electronic freezers to disable their potential opponent's weapons. One of the members of this militia was equipped with a heater to reduce any enemy into a pile of ashes and I think another was sporting a bagger weapon. It looked like the last model, a bagger weapon capable of projecting a metal snare to capture any target up to fifty-five meters away. The big guy was leading the march. His assistant, a short and thin fellow with a facial scar, was closing the march. In the front of the line I over heard the big guy finally introducing himself to my Nöel:

"I am Kemehjo, but everyone calls me Little John around here. I represent Ferika. She is very eager to meet you, Mister Clean."

"Noël, name is Noël for fuck Snakes! C'est pas possible! That Mister Clean shit is over!"

"He, he, okay Noël, chill, we are all friends here." Said the big guy.

My teammates and I were still intimidated by this militia. They were leading us higher up in the mountains. Les, a world renowned retired general and my old friend Noël Joseph the former globe trotter, did not seem to be impressed by these surroundings. Little John and Noël were still conversing in English when they suddenly switched to speaking French. When I first met Noël, I did not speak a single word of French. I had just moved from the British Isles to the BS School of Paris in New Gaul. Noël had just moved from the orphanage in Belgium to Paris the year before. We hit it off pretty quickly. One might say that it was our foreign backgrounds that started our friendship. As I mentioned before in my previous accounts, some of our classmates used to make fun of our horrible accents. Noël had a deep guttural Belgium accent and I had a fresh off the boat Islander accent. All this to say that now; I am fluent in French. But during this walk, Noël and the big guy were using a very old French lingo that I wasn't able to understand. Out of nervousness I turned to the man with the facial scar who was walking behind me. I pointed out his massive gun and I dared to ask him:

"Is this all necessary mate? All the guns and protection?"

"Yes, protection is necessary" he replied.

"Protection against what mate?" I gently inquired.

"Poachers and villains." Said the man with the facial scar. " Lots of poachers and villains around here. We protect gorillas and there are not many left around here."

"Oh fantastic," I continued" you protect gorillas?"

"Yes." Said the man while looking over his shoulder.

I decided to introduce myself.

"I'm Sam, by the way."

"Good for you." He replied. Then he slowly walked away.

I wasn't able to get much more out of him. He appeared to be on the edge, as if he was expecting something or someone to suddenly attack us. Suddenly, we all heard general Roken scream in terror:

"Mother fuckin' bug" hurled Les. " There is a giant mother fuckin' bug climbing on my mother fuckin' leg, get it off, get it offffffff!"

One of the armed guys picked up the little creature off of General Roken's pantaloons.

"Not a bug", informed the man. " t's only a little spider"

"Ahhhh, disgusting!" Les screamed frenetically. " Disgusting mother fuckin bugs!"

Every armed and unarmed member of the caravan was laughing. All except the guy with the facial scars and Les of course. My dear fiancé took a deep breath to calm down and said:

"Okay, okay, I'm good. (sniffffffff), I'm good. I'll be fine, I'm fine sorry about that".

General Lesley D. Roken is a solid killing machine. Familiar with all deadly weapons available to a man of his rank and above, issue of a military family, a celebrated general who accomplished sixty-three deadly rescue missions. A decorated General, he met many presidents and reagents around the globe. He even entertained a personal relationship with the former head of the Earthican council. Les Roken, retired from a life of intrepid dangers but he was still deadly scared of insects, arachnids and other crawling bugs. A fear that he never lost. You must imagine how funny it was to see my husky partner jumping up and down, shaking from side to side and screaming two octaves higher than usual, just because of a little bug.

After this comical interlude and an intense hike across the mountains, we found ourselves in the middle of a clearing. A camp of some sort was awaiting our arrival. A few modern tents, some larger than others, were arranged in a semi circle. The height of the mountains and the tropical isolation of this place gave us a majestic view over the valley down below. This armed militia had saved us from a supposedly dramatic end. Indeed, we should have been in the middle of the Amazon in the hands of the bloody Natural Front right now. Instead, Nöel, Zed, Babs, Les, Mehdi and I were here on top of a mountain in Central Africa. This was a neat and gorgeous place, but why drag us all the way up there?

The entire camp was protected by mean looking dogs. And a lot of em'! In front of the entrance of the largest tent, stood a guard. It was a tall lady and she was bearing a huge sword in her right hand. In the other, she was holding a striped hyena on a leash.

Once again, I could not help myself. I asked with a grin to one of the gunmen walking beside me:

"We are going in there, right?"

"Yup!" the man replied.

"Of course, we are." I told the gunman with a nervous smile.

As we entered the large tent, an old gentleman with a cane greeted us all with a generous smile and open arms and he said:

"Ladies, gentlemen and others, please sit down, your food is ready. I am M'kambé. Welcome my friends." He looked at the big guy, thank him with his eyes. And with his chin the man with the cane instructed Little John and his merry armed men to leave the tent. The man with the cane sat down and informed us:

"Little John is a good man, I recruited him as a mechanic over twenty years ago. But when I discovered that he could speak over a dozen languages I gave him a raise and he became my translator."

"What about the little scary dude?" asked Baggy.

"Oh, yes Karim? He has been with us a long time." Replied M'Kumbé. " We rescued him from Saint Bernard, the notorious war lord. Karim's parents were revered healers and animal entertainers, in this part of the world his people are known as the hyena men. But unfortunately Karim's parents were killed by Saint Bernard's men. Karim and his brother were brought to Saint Bernard as new child soldier recruits. The cruelty of Saint Bernard hiring process was simple. He only needed the most ferocious men, so he instructed the boys to turn against each other. Karim was forced to kill his brother in order to survive. A year later he tried to escape the child soldier camp. Saint Bernard's men caught him and messed up his face as a warning. When Saint Bernard finally died after a long..."

"What the hell is going on here?!!" interrupted Les with a dramatic, and commanding voice.

"Chill my brother" said the old man with the cane." We are all friends here. Our intel determined that the Natural Front was about to terminate you. We couldn't let this happen. Two more minutes and you'd be ghosts without our help. I am sorry we had to drag you all the way up here in our humble home. But since you were all drugged up we figured it was a safe bet to rescue you without first asking for your permission. You have to understand that the Mechanics and the Natural Front have been wanting to put their hands on you for quite a while."

"But the Mechanics and the Natural Front hate each other" said Mehdi. " They are in cahoots together now?"

"Impossible!" interrupted Les.

"Improbable but not impossible" said Zed." Yeah if you think about it, these two groups are basically the same thing. They are both fascists in their own sort of way. Both of these terrorist organisations are obsessed with total control and eradication of every Earthican citizen"

"Bravo! Well said" concluded the man with the cane. He paused for an instant and continued. "The NF wants total control of the earth's environment in order to protect and exploit natural resources as humans once did without the use of machines. The Mechanics them, well, they still depend on Earth's resources in order to survive, adapt and evolve. Without the Earth's natural resources and our diverse culture they cannot persist. Both organisations have recognised the flaws of their respective plans. Both The NF and the Mechanics have united to get their hand your precious agency's tech and knowledge in order to eradicate every other Earthican on the planet."

"Ok and why are you telling us this here and now?" asked Les.

"We had to bring you here." Replied the man with the cane." The NF and MX have eyes and ears everywhere. I also need to inform you that our Monitor Ferika would really like to see you and ask you a couple of questions."

"Ferry who?" asked Zed.

"Ferika, the mother of Chelone" said Noël.

To this the old man with the cane added:

"Ferika is now the tittle given to the hair of the territories of Chelone and incidentally, the last descendent of Ferika the first. Mother of modern mankind. The current Monitor of our little sanctuary has chosen to retain her name Ferika"

"Sounds pretty awesome!" said Zed.

"It is" said Noël.

Suddenly a tall and majestic woman entered the tent accompanied by a group of heavily armed guards. All of them were female guard and each of them was bearing a long and dramatic sword.

"Here she is" said M'kumbé as he placed his cane on the table."My sisters, my brothers and my others, allow me to introduce you to the Monitor of our little sanctuary : Ferika."

The gracious woman slowly sat in the chair that was especially reserved for her.

"Damn, she's hot" whispered Zed.

Ferika heard the compliment, she smiled and slightly bobbed her head as if to say; "thank you, I know". The charismatic woman started to study the faces of the team sitting around the table and suddenly stopped when she laid her eyes upon Noël:

"TRE KTE KE TEKE?" asked Ferika.

"TAKATA." my old friend replied.

I said nothing, I was a bit confused.

Apart from the man with the cane and Ferika's mighty female guardians, none of us understood the meaning of this peculiar exchange. One thing was certain, Noël knew about this place and it's inhabitants. My old friend obviously knew this woman. The situation was awkward enough for us to remain silent. Shite, it was getting pretty weird. The man with the cane whispered something in Ferika's ear, she nodded yes. Makumbé then proceeded and pointed his cane at Babs face and gently asked:

"You, grandma Kitty Cat, describe your employer, Mister Cl… Mister Noël Joseph for me please."

Babs replied with a thin voice without missing a beat:

"Compassionate, dedicated, patient?".

"No need to be nervous madam. Just wanted to have your direct opinion" Said M'kumbé. He then turned his attention to my fiancé general Les Roken and inquired:

"How did you and your employer get to work together in the first place? I am curious?"

"Noël's legal guardian and my great grandmother worked together years ago." Said Les and he continued" They kept in touch and soon after my retirement from the service my great grandmother put me in contact with Noël. Noël needed me for a job and told me that I'd be interviewed by his business partner Simon Sam Harding. They needed a competent security manager for their anti-bioterrorism business, and I got the job."

"And where is she now?" asked M'kumbé.

"My great grandmother?" said Les, a bit confused." She is resting in peace with the family in the Navajo Nation."

"And what about Noël's legal guardian, where is she now?" asked M'kumbé.

"Oh, Sister Odéna? She's in the Alps, in New Gaul." Answered Les." She lives in a monastery of some sort."

"A monastery?" inquired M'kumbé.

"A monastery, a sanctuary, I'm not sure. It's a big house in the middle of nowhere full of old folks that are reading and gardening all day."

"I see." Attested M'kumbé. The old man pointed his cane towards me and said:

"You, Sam the Islander. You are a very lucky man.

"I am?"

"Yes," he continued," You have extraordinary companions! But all good things must come to an end in order to allow the birth of new events. You see I am known, by those who are close to me; as something of a Predicator."

The man with the cane informed me that one of my friends was "the chosen one" and that that particular friend of mine was to stay here by Ferika's side. M'Kumbe also informed me that one other friend would flirt with death very soon and that a third would date lady death even sooner.

The incredible Ferika stood up, thanked us all for meeting her and she left the tent, without speaking. Zed, without warning, said her farewells and ran out the tent closely following Ferika. We were all quite confused by her running away like that but the man with the cane managed to convince us that this was for the best. As the old man had foreseen, Zed was to become Ferika's next assistant and there was nothing any of us could do about it. Once everyone else fished their meals, the man with the cane escorted us outside the tent. He then instructed Little John accompanied by his fierce looking assistant and his merry armed men to accompany our team down the mountains to the nearest airbase. The merry armed men were to keep us safe so we could fly back across the Atlantic back to our Delivery Drone. As we painfully walked our way down the rugged dirt road we were savagely attacked by an unknown assailant

(BOOM!)

A brutal detonation exploded, and everything went dark.

## 31 A TRUE WARAL IS CONSTANTLY LEARNING AND TEACHING.

Learning and teaching the comforting words to accompany ceremonies. Email sent to a fellow Waral enthusiast composed by Dr. Muriel Lanaide in March 2031 AD. (Distributed in the year Alpha three point eleven)

From: doctormurriela@northennewgauluniversity.obs to professorrenettolini@northennewgauluniversity.obs

Dear Professor Renettolini, I am very pleased to tell you that not only I have received the books you sent me but I have just finished them.

During our last conversation you suggested that the followers of the Waral way of life view themselves as a scientific and philosophical group of independent individuals more than a spiritual group. Yet I am starting to think that some of these Warals apply an almost religious method regarding some of their celebratory events marking the passage from a life to an other or some other celebration welcoming a new person or a new step in one's life. Allow me to quote you some of the passages that I regard as deeply spiritual and almost religious.

Births: Tre Kte Ke Téné! Takata Kumpa! Téné Téné Té.

The amount of lives given to form your existence. Oh my globe, this globe is yours. One day you may choose one path or another. You may want to learn as much as you may want to learn. For now you have a world to explore and your close ones have a duty to nurture, educate and protect you. Ask and we will teach you, give and you will learn. We have to celebrate together all the possibilities that existence has to offer. You! Born during the season of the heat you are encouraged by the fire, the hottest of all elements. You! Born during the season of the harvest your life is now till the end of time driven by this bond between you and the earth, the most determinant element of all. You! Born during the rainy season you have been given a gift, the gift of life and continuity, the water will carry you as it is the element of growth and strength. You! Born during the season conducted by the winds of change, your life is now in the hands of your own breeze.

Celebration/Union : Tre Kte Ke Teke! Takata Kumpa! Téké Tet Téké

You must thank the lives burrowed to guide your route. You must look back. Look at your achievements, we are here to share and celebrate your feat. But your journey is not over, for a true Waral is constantly learning and teaching. You have allowed this gathering, we must liberate and convene, we must celebrate as the sun will flash the moon with a sparkling beam. You! And You! Have chosen to unite, you have decide to join your lives and build an existence shared with your close relatives. Your union/your celebration/your future or past walkabout/is a festivity that none of us will forget. For you/and you, are in our hearts, in our minds and in our files. We are all gathered here today to experience the union/the celebration/the walkabout/that you are about to celebrate with us with the globe, full of existence and grace, will provide with countless offerings. We must admire your totem, your sign, your animal spirit or spirits if you chose to do so. In any case the four elements of existence will accompany your journey.

Memorium: Tre Kte Ke Pati

Our duty is to honour your life, we must respect that the recycling of your life is an integral part of existence. No departure should provoke such emotion. A departure, at any age, is not easy to accept. All these lives given to form yours, reclaimed and resting peacefully upon the shoulders of the Earth. Your life consumed by the globe, feeding our tears, the same tears feeding the earth, your death is part of life, and soon the next generation will be inspired to give birth. Your existence is celebrated today as part of the cycle of life. Many celebrations, unions, births, walkabouts, graduations and other ceremonies have taken place here where we stand today. But the celebration of your existence is exceptional, it has never been nor will ever be conducted again. We must accept your decisions, your achievements and your departure as much as we have a duty to celebrate the joy of having sharing our lives with a small part of your entire existence. You have taught us so much that we must honour your gifts and continue to teach the values of your existence.

## 32 FOLLOWING THE WARAL WAY OF LIFE AND STEPPING INTO A SANCTUARY IS A CHOICE.

Wanderers in search of a refuge, by Jekano Almecia. Discovered by the third Anonymous scribe in early 1861 AD. Original copy owned by the Warality museum in Bruevanilio, Central America (On display since the year Alpha four point zero)

Warals and visitors, stepping into a Sanctuary in search of a refuge of a possible residency.

Ye who will hear this message, ye who will receive this invitation.

To all individuals stepping into our domain in search of peace and direction.

Ye who fled the claws of slavery, ye who ran away from your conquered city.

To all those following the Waral way of life or not ,our domain will provide protection.

Thou who has chosen to enter and to retire in our humble Sanctuary.

You stepping away from the monstrosities and genocides forced upon you without an invitation.

Ye who is simply looking for a refuge and a meal and ye seeking the path towards Warality.

To all wanderers and roamers of the lands, to those who desire to heal with determination.

Ye who fought and will fight once more, ye who seek a piece of mind with serenity.

Ye who doesn't not follow the path, even your wounds can heal without hesitation.

All are welcome in our Sanctuary, from a short passage to full residency.

As our global human tribe is confined to explosive fractions and distortion.

Warals and visitors alike will always remain under the nurturing graces of Warality.

Tell them that following the path of the Waral way of life and stepping into a Sanctuary is a choice.

## 33 THE WARALS ACKNOWLEDGE THE NATURAL AND ORGANIC RECYCLING PROCESS OF LIFE AND DEATH. THEY RECOGNISE THAT LIFE AND DEATH ARE TWO DIFFERENT SIDES OF THE SAME PROCESS OF EXISTENCE.

Letter of resignation from the order of St Francis of Saint Bacoutti, Central Africa. Letter from Sister Odéna to the mother superior. Original manuscript owned and translated by the Fearful scribe. (Distributed early in the year Alpha four point one)

Letter of resignation of the order of Saint Francis to Mother Superior from Sister Odéna:

Mother Superior and my fellow Sisters of the order, I have come to the conclusion that I will always remain a sister of our great order of Saint Francis but I have failed to feel the call and the touch of the deity behind the throne sitting in Rome. For I will always revere our Natural visionary and preacher of Assisi I can no longer answer to the demands of any deity. As you know I have fled my birth place in search of life stripped of all crowned demands. For I will no longer answer the call of regality I feel I must therefore divorce myself from divine commands.

I have to forward my acknowledgement of the only force able to dictate my every move; existence. For it is the only force able to provide me with the tools to help me operate by the prowess of my own person. I regret to inform you that I must break my vows in search of the elucidating mysteries attributed to what is known by the followers of the Waral way of life as; existence. The Warals acknowledge the natural and organic recycling process of life and death. They recognise that life and death are two different sides of the same process of existence. This is a message that profoundly speaks to me. From now on I refuse to fear death and will no longer pursue a career gravitating around half lives. I am convinced that our lives and our deaths are but different sides of the coin that is existence. I desire to preserve cordial relations with your church and I will always conserve enough time to work with the orphanage.

Mother superior will concede and accept my resignation, my wishes and demands will be forwarded by the Scribe of Sanctuary of the Chocolate for I have found repose and refuge at this extraordinary place of harmony, learning and exploration. Mother superior will find the courage and the audacity to welcome my personal choices and will, I hope, will accept the invitation as a visitor and a fellow Sister of Francis to visit me in my new home at the Sanctuary.

## 34 EACH WARAL WHO DECIDES TO MAKE USE OF THE ESSENTIAL BLOOM MUST MAKE IT BLOOM PERSONALLY UNLESS PHYSICALLY UNABLE TO DO SO.

Legends of the four sisters. Auction of the copy of a partial tablet dating from the late 14th century AD. Artefact rediscovered on August 21st 1946 AD. Transcript recovered and translated by the Scribe of blue Willows. (Published in the year Alpha four point nine)

-Tock, tock, tock! (explicit banging of the gavel)

-Silence, please. Ladies, gentlemen and others. As the host of this auction I have the pleasure of presenting today a copy of the ancient Tablets translated and recovered by Mrs. Maud. This artefact, this rare and expensive artefact, is an exact copy of the tablet containing the legends of the four sisters. As you may or may not know the agronomic and agricultural applications of plants called sisters has been detailed by some of the reputable original American historians. The appearance of a method known as the three sisters, notably the simultaneous growth of corn, pssifoquoii, beans, ditipoquoii and tomatoes, tissiquoii, is now regarded as one of the most advanced botanical balance of all times. I am glad to present for auction today this perfectly preserved tablet exposing the secrets behind the cultivation of the fourth sister, the essential bloom.

-Tock, tock, tock! (soft banging of the gavel to keep the audience riveted)

-Please, allow me to continue. I will now read a small passage from this exquisite and valuable object.

-Tock, tock,tock! (a man wants to speak, but his word is denied)

-Sir if you want to contemplate and feel this artefact you are going to have to wait, or you have to purchase the item immediately, double the price! Well, I didn't think so. Now, I trust that none of you will interrupt my reading;

Warals, wanderers, walkers and roamers seeking healing, nourishment, enlightenment and garments. The fourth sister provided by mother nature and perfected by mankind will be therefore given to the followers of the Waral way of life all forms, entrusted with sacred and philosophical goals, should make the fourth sister bloom for themselves and others. The first sister was meant to provide beans for your people and a rich foliage to feed the second sister. As the second sister grew, its impressive proportions were attended and sculpted by mankind; as a way to harvest grains and provide a solid structure to welcome the arrival of the third sister. Providing pulpous and fleshy fruits, the third sister was considered to be an extraordinary gift, but one more sister was to be added to the sisterhood of natural delights. The fourth sister, generously offered by the fertile lands of the descendants of Attam and Assam, has travelled all over the globe. From the isles of Komorh to the land of Ferika, the fourth sister has now joined our blooming agriculture. Roamers have developed varieties of the fourth sister that allow the rest of us to protect our bodies from the harsh elements. Walkers have chosen a different route, for they have given us a fourth sister with a foliage so large that only one specimen can feed an entire family. Wanderers have given us a fourth sister that can provide medicine to treat the most virulent conditions. The Warals have been travelling and cultivating their own way of life for hundreds of thousands of years, and since then, they have roamed our beautiful Earth spreading the virtues of the essential bloom. I must add that, originally, according to old traditions, each Waral who decides to make use of the essential bloom must make it bloom personally unless physically unable to do so.

This essential bloom, known to us as the fourth sister is now an integral part of the Waral way of life in some form or another. After years of trials and errors, a small group of Warals agreed on a simple guidance concerning the mind altering variety of the fourth sister. This mind altering variety was to be treated with respect and dignity. This essential bloom had a mild effect compared to beverages and other mind altering devices, but its effects could be doubled and tripled with the proper tending. So this small group of followers of the Waral way of life decided that each of them who decides to make use of the essential bloom must make it bloom personally unless physically unable to do so. This guidance, or tradition, has grown exponentially over the years. In effect, growing and making use of the fourth sister with mind altering properties also known as the essential bloom by the followers of the Waral way of life is regarded as an artistic, agronomic, logical and philosophical activity.

## 35 THE WARALS HONOUR BOTH THE WRATH AND THE GENEROSITY OF FERIKA. THEY REGARD FERIKA AS BOTH THE MOTHER OF MODERN MANKIND AND THE MOTHERLAND OF MANKIND.

"A new political weather". Speech given by Lenate Juakanu before his assassination in 2067 AD. Generously translated by Mrs. Mannie. Original manuscript owned by the library of the Sanctuary of Tranquillus, Eurasia. (On display since the year Alpha four point ten)

The end of complicity and obscenity is over,

As you may have heard, some of my most ravenous competitors have sent their favourite crows to deliver an undermining and troubling message. These crows have congratulated me for gathering such an impressive political support, but they are clear; they want to divide and share my followers amongst themselves. They want to leave me behind, and they want me to consider a dusty bribe. A tiny bribe nonetheless.

Do you think I should accept their dusty bribe? Do you truly think I would allow my fervent admirers being taken away from me? Do you think I would allow my supporters to be dispatched, separated and dismissed of a voice? Allas we have lands to tend to, fields to fertilise within reason, families to feed, children need better education, scientists deserved to be allowed to pursue unbiased research for they only desire to enrich our culture independently of the domination of a perverted government. We have an incalculable number of engineers, philosophers, artists and individuals craving to expose the world as they see it.

As you may or may not know, I think it is time for our constituents to revive and regulate the ever growing legislation hatched by our ineffective government as much as the population in dire need to be kept off the leash in the hands of ineffective and lawless regulators. Our society must be allowed to grow up and finally become responsible and reasonable. Every resident of our great society must be allowed to breathe as much as our government needs to live up to the expectations of the same individuals who vote them into office in the first place.

I am not like other politicians, I am not going to lie to you and tell you that I am a traditional family man with a wise and kids, I am not going to try to convince you that I am a perfect individual who is never wrong, I am not going to convince you that I am not a politician and will certainly not finish my speech by promising you impossible things. For you see, I am politician, I have a husband but no kids, when I am corrected, I accept the criticism with grace and my pleasures a much less expensive than golf, champagne, roaring cars and private hotels. If you want to know who I really am, feel free to visit my farm for lunch. Thereafter I will show you the vegetable garden and we can start happy hour early in the music room.

Some of you are not yet familiar with my program. Let me start by expressing that my program contains no promises, I promise nothing! I can only guarantee that I will enter the political arena to fight for personal liberty, individual freedom and property, the right to advocate old and new methods to help our society flourish and bloom better and stronger than ever. I can only guarantee that a new era of cooperation and social justice is on the verge of being born. I can only guarantee the encouragement of new and old methods of distraction and entertainment. I can only guarantee a diminution and a responsible repartition of our taxes. At the same time I can only guarantee that private, public and independent enterprises will receive the proper respect and admiration they deserve.

You see, I make no promises. I will not magically fix any of your problems, not a single one. For you see I do not believe in problems, I only believe in solutions, in reconciliation. And this is why I am pleased to tell you that I have sent the crows of my competitors back to where they came with a reply to their message of indignation and bribery: You cannot stop a small man from building something great, I will continue to build with my meagre means and more supporters will join me. For they are tired of you!

We have so many beautiful faiths and beliefs that deserve an equal recognition and we also have incredible minds who are focused on their work and proud of their atheism. So many folkloric traditions and modern ceremonies deserve to be alleviated and recognised. As for me I follow the path of the Waral way of life. I honour the wrath and the generosity of Ferika and the concept of existence. I regard Ferika as the mother of mankind as much as I esteem that Ferika is the motherland of our human existence.

I have studied your needs and I want to deliver justice. I have studied my competitors and I was able to think like them in order to bypass their nonsense. I was forced to study myself and my own needs, it was absolutely necessary to be honest with myself. This helped me realise what makes me; ME. I encourage you to do the same, make the effort to figure out what your neighbour wants, determine the objective of your opponents and analyse what they need and finally but most importantly you have to ask yourself honestly; what about me? This my friends, is an old decisive method the Warals call the Yu De Mi method, or you them me analysis. Use my recommendations wisely, for they belong to you now.

The age of hypocrisy and double standards must come to an end. Our society is in dire need of military reforms to secure our defence department to operate efficiently. We need the creation of medical and social reforms accessible to all classes. We have countless sources of medicine and pleasure that need to be properly structured and available. Our government must be held accountable for the drive of our society, taxes need to be lowered and re distributed intelligently. New states must be encouraged to join our unique united and constitutional structure. We have to encourage the development of multicultural and international agreements.

Thank you so much for being here today. One law, one love. We must… (bang)

## 36 THE WARALS MUST ASSIST ANY PERSON IN NEED.

Passage from "the Epic poems of poisons", ratified in 1532 AD. Discovered and translated by the Scribe of Dawn in 2029 AD. Relic donated to the Library of Congress located in Washington D.C. in North America. (On display since the year Alpha five point one)

The value of intuitive and inquisitive behaviour to counter terror. Why feeding and lodging those in need is primordial. (Alpha five point one)

" As you will discover, the Warality can be attained in many ways. Those who decide to follow the path of the Waral way of life may decide to reside in a Sanctuary, they may as well live their entire existence without stepping into one. All share a deep connection with the earth and all the organisms that are the completion or our beautiful globe. Every Waral must assist any person in need. This important article is rarely misinterpreted. In fact all Sanctuaries are prepared to receive guests and all Wilders, or lonely Walkers, are ready to share a portion of their meals. All medicine and agricultural needs should be at the disposition of a guest, it is customary to introduce the guest to other visitors and residents. A tour of the Sanctuary, or property, or domain, or territory is encouraged. For you see this book contains all the recipes that are needed to exploit the wonders of our natural world. Unfortunately some individuals with good or bad intentions have been using secrets contained in chapters included in this book of poisons. It is advised to destroy or at least edit this book, for the greater good. All recipes and methods are present in other literary works. The danger of this book is that it contains all the deadliest recipes as well as all medicinal remedies.It should be agreed that only medicinal recipes have a valid importance. You find it useful and more practical to copy and reproduce recipes with beneficial values. The modern world should not be exposed to the detrimental recipes present in this book. A follower of the Waral way of life must be able to feed and lodge any person in need. If a guest were to find the original version of the book of poisons, a great mystery would certainly cloud the future of mankind. If a lonely Walker should assist and nurture a person in need, this Waral should be morally and ethically inclined to provide assistance, as fruitful or simplistically as possible."

## 37 ANY WARAL INVITING VISITORS IN A SANCTUARY MUST BE RESPONSIBLE FOR SAID VISITORS.

Telegram accompanied by an estimate and a cover letter dating from December 3rd 1865 AD. addressed to the Sanctuary of the Quelebs. Translated by T.R.W. Ferrond in the year Alpha five point one. (Published in the year Alpha five point two)

Dear Madam Peterillio, you will find the estimate that you have requested as well as a telegram delivered this morning validating your demand to proceed to the construction of your establishment; noted the Sanctuary of the Quelebs. I have received a formal demand from the Governor of our immense territory, asking that, at your convenience of course, a banquet shall take place once your establishment is up and running. Your strange and exotic way of life has sparked interest amongst a handful of my colleagues and we are honoured to accept your invitation. As you mentioned during our first interview; any person visiting a Sanctuary must be under the responsibility of one of its residents. I can assure you that our conduct will be exemplary as we are quite joyous to learn more about your studies and practices. Please feel free to respond in time and will start the paperwork process in order to grant you the privilege of establishing your Sanctuary. I regard our partnership with great admiration and I remain at your service. L.D.Z. Ferrond, solicitor for the Grand territories estates.

Sanctuary admitted. Stop. Deposit cashed in. stop. Bylaws of the Sanctuary of the Quelebs validated by the highest authority. Stop. Since no external investment or debt the establishment can pursue at once. Stop. Carry on with signature. Response is expected from all parties involved. Stop.

Estimate for the creation of the Sanctuary of the Quelebs, Island of Quelebs, Greater territories:

Price and location of the property: $460, Island of Quelebs part of the jurisdiction of the Greater territories.

Building process and cost: to be established immediately and to be funded by diverse donations. The land purchased by the council of the Quelebs is now under their responsibility. The building or buildings as well as storage facilities, fields and the forest surrounding the Sanctuary is to be maintained by the Sanctuary. All expenses and matters at hand can be viewed and reviewed by the officers of the Greater territories and any person welcomed to stay in the Sanctuary or any individual who choses to visit the Sanctuary unannounced will be assisted, fed and helped as gracefully as possible. Taxation of such an establishment is not advisable for its purpose is not commercial, nor profitable. The Sanctuary must be treated with dignity like any other charitable establishment and shall exchanges must be handled accordingly.

Supervision and expectations: the domain supervised by talented architects, doctors and natural scientists. The Sanctuary is expecting to produce enough resources to achieve self reliance before the end of the year. A surplus of goods is expected to be re distributed and donated through charitable processes inside and outside of the Greater territories.

When a follower of the Waral way of life invites an individual, this Waral must be responsible for the wellbeing of said visitor. Visitors are treated with admiration and tended with ever loving care. No visitor should feel disappointed to have entered a Sanctuary, visitors must be considered with great care. No visitor should feel too cold, no visitor should feel too hot. No visitor should go hungry of thirsty, no visitor should be plagued by fatigue and stress. If a visitor is in need of medical assistance, this assistance shall be provided immediately. If a visitor is in need of a guide or a companion, the Sanctuary shall do everything it can to provide it within the limits of possibilities and dignity.

Rentability and mission: the Sanctuary is not oriented towards profit or fame, it is meant to be an establishment revolving around abundance and wisdom. The mission is to welcome any individual of any tribe, of any continent, of any personal and spiritual preference that is of age. The age of majority is determined by the land upon which the Sanctuary is established.

Notes: tax exemption as agreed upon the sale of one of the parcel(s) on the island of Queleb, location of this parcel is on the eastern part of the island. As agreed upon, the surrendered parcel of the island will not be subjected to the legislature existing on the continent. The parcel will be the site of the Fort of Queleb, under the jurisdiction of the governor of the Greater northern territories.

## 38 A WARAL SANCTUARY IS OPEN TO ANY VISITOR, HATCHLING AND WARAL.

Passage from an article first published in October 1951 AD by Historian Magazine. Conversation translated by the Scribe of the Blooms late in the year Alpha four point nine. (Distributed in April of the year Alpha five point four)

Passage about the conversation between the wise one and the wild one. Talk about the importance, or non importance of the Sanctuary, talk about the taboos, rituals and the importance, or non importance given to signs, gris-gris and other totems.

The Wise: Thank you for this introduction, I just want to say that my friend and I are pleased to give this little talk together.

The Wilder: We ain't friends.

Laugh in the audience.

The Host: Well, thank you both, now we have some questions from the audience I hope you will answer. First question is about Sanctuaries. Miss Flaura is asking how important are these sanctuaries for the followers of the Waral way of life.

The Wise: It is very simple, you see every community and every institutions are allowed to regroup under the same roof and adhere to the beliefs of their own choice. Some Sanctuaries established in some of the most remote places are equipped with up to date technologies, some on the other hand are very rustic and traditional. Some establishments contain a multitude of complex buildings and others are very modest dwellings. The importance of a Sanctuary is in the eye of the one who desires to step in a Sanctuary. These establishment provide filing quarters, meals, clean water, amenities and a series of spaces available for residents and visitors to explore what they desire the most. For example, some Sanctuaries are very important because they have educational programs available for all, Warals and non Warals alike. I want to remind everybody that a Waral sanctuary is open to any visitor, hatchling and Waral. We have libraries and workshops of all shapes and sizes. To tell you the truth some establishments are under contract with the local authorities to conduct research and development programs, others serve as art galleries, music studios and theatres. You see these Sanctuaries are important for some of us and I am convinced that...

The Wilder: What he is trying to say is that not all Sanctuaries are the same, everybody can find a perfect Sanctuary for oneself. I do not share this feeling but that is just me. My entire life is a Walkabout, I like to hike, camp and travel with the seasons. Now, that is just me. I'm a Wilder but I know other Wilders who reside in Sanctuaries, shit, even some of them are mono Sanctuaries.

The Host; mono-Sanctuaries?

The Wise: Yes, these are Sanctuaries created by one Waral for one Waral.

The Wilder: Yeah, they live alone, far from everything and still they alway prepare enough food for eventual guests. Even if nobody ever pays them a visit.

The Host: Oh dear, that is... a lonely life.

The Wise: Yes, but it is a happy life. You have to understand that every Waral has a different vision of the world, that is the beauty of it. Some of us feel the need to build together, we must respect the wishes of those who seek solitude and remoteness. Respect is a very important part of our way of life.

The Host: Your religion is, I must say fascinating and I do believe that...

The Wilder: The fuck? Not a religion; a way of life. A religion is dogmatic and has rules and degenerates into madness and genocide.

The Wise: Some of us regard our philosophy as a religion it is true but a religion without deities and supernatural intervention...

The Host: I see, and how do all Warals agree on anything then?

The Wilder: that is the trick, we almost never agree on the details but we all have the same aim.

The Host: And that would be?

The Wise: That would be our unique and only law. One law; one love. That is why all Sanctuaries, mono-Sanctuaries and huts, like the one my friend live in, is ready to welcome any person in need but visitors and hatchlings are encouraged to discover how the followers of the Waral way of life chose to pursue their existence. In harmony with an incredible…

The Wilder: Once again we are not friends. But I must agree that our goal is to be a peaceful and helpful community.

The Wise: Yes, even my rude non-friend here, is prepared to go the extra mile. The Warals have been taking care of each other for generations. In times of wars, famine and desperation, our elders have always welcomed strangers with open arms.

The Wilder: We are a rare bunch of folks and we respect all other bunch of folks. We do not have taboos or forbidden practices. We are free spirited, you know.

The Host: I see, that is interesting. Are the Warals vegetarians?

The Wilder: Fuck no we have a….

The Wise: What my rude non friend here is trying to say is that we do not have dietary requirements. Some Warals are in fact pure vegetarians but they are a minority. Most Warals eat a little bit of everything, meat, fish, shellfish you name it. And since most of us have a green thumb, we have fresh produce available at all times. Look, the path to Warality is riddled with intricacies, any person of any locality, or social background and any sexual preference has the right to follow this way of life. We do not have taboos and interdictions, we are relatively simple. Unlike a certain number of philosophies out there, our way of life is strictly against killing, raping and stealing. It is that simple.

The Wilders: I have to agree with my fr… college here. The Warals are opposed to brutality, inequality and inequity. We only want to be left alone so we can do our thing you know.

The Host: Your thing?

The Wise: Yes, gardening, reading, studying history, teaching, acting, fencing, playing the cello. Whatever make you happy, you should just do it.

The Host: As long as it is non violent right?

The Wilder: Well, one should be allowed and encouraged to box, but only against another boxer. Violence is a natural process, but it has to be channeled, diligently.

The Host: I… guess so.

The Wise: Yes, well concerning the place of violence in the deck of cards of life, one should be prepared. We are against brutality and violence in general but that doesn't mean that we do not channel our energy emotions.

The Wilder: If you are a Waral and you need to blow off some steam go play drums, or run very fast or start a friendly boxing match with a mate that's what I say. But free brutality, no sir. That is unacceptable.

## 39 THE WARAL WAY OF LIFE REGARDS THAT THE RESPECT AND WORSHIP OF NATURE IS NATURAL INDEED.

Passages from the journal of the Weightless Scribe started in the late 21st century. Manuscript discovered and published by Dr. Reignakov, a Waral history enthusiast. Original kept at the publisher's home. (Published in the year Alpha five point six)

Third of may 2025: Back from a vigorous talk with the boss. Tired of this shit. What's the point of spending time and energy for this crooked company anyway?

Not worth my pay check. Tired of this flat. This city is going bonkers. I have lost my faith in this fucked up country, I need to see the world.

Seventeenth of October 2026: Attended this year's philosophy and theology convention near Addis Ababa, had a wonderful time. Had the opportunity to chat with ministers, rabbis, imams, bishops, pagan druids, Wiccan priestesses and a strange group of nature worshippers who call themselves the Warals. They say that they follow the path of Warality, a path that cannot be dictated by divine nor regal intervention. Was invited to learn more about them.

Nineteenth of October 2027: Extraordinary thing happened today. I fell in love again, in love with the world. My new Waral friends gave me shelter, food and introduced me to their beliefs. Living in a large capital for over twenty years made me blind to the wonders of the natural world, my new friends helped me realise that. Asked them why I have never heard of their strange community before. They replied: 'we do not conduct crusades, nor do we try to convert anybody. We roam and campaign and whoever listens, listens'. These campaigns allow the followers of the Waral way of life to walk the Earth and spread their message of love for the natural world. They regard the respect for natural world to be natural indeed.

Year Alpha zero point one: Since the fall of the Monster, the members of the newly elected Earthican Council is trying to convince the rest of the world that the authors of the atrocities perpetrated by the Natural Front have been taken into custody. My friends and I have petitioned the government to warn them about this new terrorist organisation since the early 2000s. The Scribe of our Sanctuary has found evidence that the Natural Front has tried to infiltrate our Waral community repetitively. It appears that this group is trying to acquire the book of poisons. Glad that they will never get their hands on it since it no longer exists.

Year Alpha zero point thirteen: Got the chance to finish my second walkabout. The Warals are deeply spiritual and they all share an exquisite love for history, that is why I have decided to learn how to become a Scribe in the hope of maybe, one day, construct my own Sanctuary. We must remain neutral and expose the brutal history of mankind as it is. These are extremely important attributes. Once the vision is completed, a follower may initiate a walkabout. Once the Walkabout comes to an end, one may feel the need to construct a project, a goal, a building, an enterprise. Whatever the form of construction chosen, one may be asked why following this way of life is of the utmost importance. Some may wonder what the Waral way of life is all about. To attain Warality one must be prepared to answer any questions. Especially during a Walkabout, since during this particular activity, the follower of the Waral way of life is in search of the right path. During these voyages, one may be compelled to spread this exquisite way of life. An elder once said; " we do not conquer with their arms, we campaign with our philosophy". There is a ring of truth to this statement. The fact that the Waral way of life still remains relatively obscure and often misinterpreted by the outside world proves that this way of life is not pushy. The life of a Waral revolves around a poetic worship of nature.

Year Alpha one point one: The Natural Front are a dangerous group led by misguided individuals. They are completely opposed to technology and they are viewed as the exact opposite of the Mechanical Forces living above the skies in their fancy space stations. At least the Mechanix are not trying to sabotage everything here down on Earth. Sympathisers of the Natural Front live in remote areas, most of them are survivalists and they take extreme measures. They have vowed to exterminate every follower of the Waral way of life as well as any civilian refusing to join them. The Natural Front is keep on destroying anything that stands in their way to accomplish their sinister goal: plunge humanity back into the stone age, even if that means using the most technologically advanced weaponry available.

Year Alpha five point five: Officer Linee dropped by for a sip and a chat. He is very pleased with my Sanctuary. He is particularly fond of our respect for legislative and representative actions taken by our establishment. He wanted to thank us all personally for all the wonderful work we achieved to keep our humble County safe, educated and clean. We told him it was an honour to volunteer and help out the best we can. Officer Linee has informed me that a handful of conspiracy theorists are desperate to put the Warals and the Natural Front in the same category. He was kind enough to suggest that we should be careful of possible attempts on our lives by the Front and other wacky conspiracy theorists. I reminded him that we never make use of violence but we are always prepare for a potential conflict.

Year Alpha five point six: I am getting old and frail. About to start yet another Walkabout, cannot get enough of these exquisite journeys. I will probably campaign until the day I die. If anybody asks about me, tell them I had a wonderful life.

## 40 THE WARALS BELIEVE IN THE CYCLE OF LIFE AND DEATH THAT IS EXISTENCE AND THEY SERVE NATURE.

The papyrus of Silence, composed by the Silent one in 154 BC. Translated by Jim Hakoopeakua, presidential historian and Voynich manuscript expert. Relic on display at the Smithers History Museum of Springfield,

North America. (Document first published in the year Alpha five point seven)

If you are slow, be strong like the tortoise and use patience to your advantage.

If you are mighty, be like the tallest elephant and protect the rest of the herd, that is your duty.

If you can fly, be like the falcon and warn off dangers.

If you are resilient, be like the hyena, be positive and clean up the lands.

If you are sharp, be like the monitor lizard, be sensitive to the surroundings to prevent dangers.

Every animal has a specialty, you must learn from at least one of them.

If you treat the guide well, the code of the path will become clear.

A woman is in love, she wants to introduce her new man to her father. In doing so she decides to invite her tender half and six other men for dinner. The woman tells her father that he can guess who her new lover is, but only after the meal. Once everybody has broken the fast, the woman helps her father in the kitchen. At this point the woman asks: " so, father, can you guess which one of these men is my man?" The father replies " is it the one in the blue shirt?" The woman, surprised, asks: " how did you guess?" The father says: " because I don't like him". Morality, one cannot please everyone all the time.

A good assistant will do half your job, a bad assistant will give you twice as much work.

They say that in the jungle all animals live together, but some animals live separate from the rest.

They also say that in the village, free trade is free, for those who can afford it.

In the South they celebrate the summer in the winter, in the North they celebrate winter in the summer. I only say that because I like in a very central area.

You must realise that life and death is only a matter of perspective from existence itself. The deer lives a long life until the hunter does his job. Once the creature is eaten and all the parts are recycled into leather, ropes, glue, and soup, one of the bones may be used by the hunter. This exceptional bone is cleaned and perhaps cried into a flute? After the meal a song may be sung, a poem may be recited, a dance may be considered. But where is the deer after such a treatment? Some part became food for those who eat meat, other parts are used for essential materials, even by those who do not eat meat, and all the while a song is performed by the flutist. The essence of the deer is still alive. The family is well fed, well entertained and kept safe from the elements. You see, existence is greater than life or death, everything changes, everything evolves to preserve what the Warals call existence. You see the Warals believe in the cycle of life and death that is existence, and they serve nature because we are all part of it.

One must learn how to turn the page before flying into a rage.

You never know when inspiration will strike you in the back, or on the side.

If you get the guide you'll get the code!

## 41 TO ATTAIN WARALITY ONE MUST GO THROUGH THREE DISTINCT PHASES; A VISION, A WALKABOUT AND FINALLY A PHASE OF CONSTRUCTION.

Section four and a half of the cylinders of Pahh, discovered on November 4th 1798 AD. Translated and published by the second Lonely scribe. Partial artefact kept at the museum of Carlota Mañana in Mexico, Central America. (On display since the year Alpha five point thirteen)

You may have seen them roam the lands and keep it clean, but there are so many that you haven't seen. From the wise Elders, the most senior walkers, to the curious hatchlings of all ages, all those who follow the natural laws represented by love, desires and ambitions of all sizes have one thing in common; they agree on one law; one love. A wilder you may have set your eyes upon, without even realising it. Living surrounded by nature and nourished by meditation, without distilled artifice. Immobile and monitoring the landscape, the Wilders are everywhere but rare are those who desire to be seen. The roamers, living off the gifts of nature and man. Accepting food, hydration and shelter when offered. Unlike most Wilders, the roamers have more manners and their journey is, more often than so, temporary. The walkers are easily spotted as they follow a route leading them to discover what their now walkabout is all about. You see them all the time, especially when the weather is sublime. All those who follow the Waral way of life have been walkers at some point or another, some like to walk so much that it has become a second nature. They have a passion for their nomadic lifestyles. As for the primordials, they were considered sacred, essentials and sage. Any Waral has a personal duty to protect the primordials. The residents are those who decide to live in sanctuaries. They feel a certain attachment towards these places of healing and learning, most of them aspire to teach, others want to construct, others want to become scribes, figures, treasurers or monitors. Some Warals belong to no particular branch, they consider that they are a part of all branches. All share the same desire to attain a state of Warality, or ultimate wisdom. And to attain Warality one must go through three distinct phases; a vision, a walkabout and finally a phase of construction

This way of life is riddled with mysteries that only you can elucidate. If the Codex can be redacted and distributed, then it will understood above ground. If so, then the loot will be found. If the Codex can be shared, then our way of life may be spared. To attain Warality is a precious thing. Being responsible and at peace, without having to endure the agony and the orders delivered by regality and so called deity.

The eternals are surprisingly long lived, Nadiana for example...

-data missing-

## 42 (THE LATEST ARTICLE) THE WARALS ACKNOWLEDGE THAT HUMANITY HAS A RARE GIFT; INTROGRESSION.

Introgression: an Earthican method. Partial document started by Noël Joseph. Completed, edited and published by the Last Scribe. Original manuscript kept in archives of the Sanctuary of La Chocolatine in Northern New Gaul. (Published in the year Alpha Six point Zero)

Abstract: Introgression is a term used to describe a biological phenomenon present in virtually every organism. In the following segments, introgression will be exposed, pulled apart and will be subjected to a philosophical dissection in order to transpose the word Introgression from a biological point of view into a simple method to analyse and determine our existence. Once the term Introgression will enter the vernacular world, every single Earthican citizen will then be able to determine what is the exact nature and composition of their own beings. From sourcing localities to determine the importance of mixed techniques and sociocultural determinations, Introgression, as a mechanical methodology, should be able to answer more questions than it generates questions. It is nowadays commonly believed that time-space, matte-rgy, non-linear progression of events have become overrated phenomenons. The following paper will attempt to demonstrate the importance of introgression as a real and palpable methodology.

Look within yourself, ask yourself where you are from, where do your ancestors come from. Ask yourself who and what you are. By using introgression as a methodology, all will be able to discover that our introgressive journey is nothing but a shared experience. A journey that divides as much as it unites us as a species. Dear reader, don't be afraid to look inwards and explore your own introgressive journey. Each of us has a unique journey, itself guided by specific code. Each code must be personally cracked. My code is the following:

Origin unknown, orphan heritage shared by all.

Never forget the mother of modern mankind.

Each of us is linked by humanity

Observe, learn, miscalculate, commit mistakes and gain experience

Two hand to move of, two eyes to see beyond

Dare to ruffle feathers in a friendly manner

Opt for the wisest solution, not the safest, for nothing is safe

Guarantee a certain amount of love in your life

Watch the skies, for they are watching you

One can forgive

One can never really forget

Drive your desires with passion

Demote your self conscious pretension

Remember who and what you are

Mingle with friends and opponents alike, for all may teach you something new

Don't forget to give

Use your imagination

Summon your inner beauty, it lies under a tree

Always acknowledge that humanity has a rare gift; the gift of introgressive thinking. Accept that each individual is a collection of mysteries and intrigues and all are bearers of a code that awaits to be cracked. You'll be surprised when you will finally discover who and what you really are. And most importantly where you come from.

# V Introgression:

When I came through, I was laying in a bed at the Bethesda military hospital near Washington D.C. My fiancé as well as my teammates were all around me. But Zed and Noël were missing. I was informed that right after the explosion, my friends woke up and managed to pull my unconscious arse to safety. Once safe, the merry armed men as well as my old friend disappeared in the forest to hunt down our assailants. Noël and Little John never returned.

A strange parcel wrapped in a bright orange ribbon waiting for me next to me on the nightstand. I opened it. The parcel contained a thick stack of papers. The first piece of paper on top of the stack was a letter addressed to me:

"Sam, you will find a collection of my personal research. It contains all the Waral articles and stories that I have managed to gather over the years. Where I am going, I have no use for it. You are the most trustworthy person I have ever known. When we met in Paris years ago, I was fresh out of the orphanage and you had just moved from Cranky Island. The fact that we remained friends all these years means the world to me. I have taught you everything I know, but you have taught me so much more! I have absolute confidence that you will be able to finish translating my research about the introgressive method and the Waral history. I want you, no I need you to publish it. Take your time, be patient. The world needs to know the truth about those who follow the Waral way of life. Zed is in excellent hands; she will finally be able to realise her biggest dreams. I am going to miss working with Babs, she was such a ball of sunshine. We had so much fun together. Please tell Judith and Mehdi that I know everything about their affair. I guess I should have known better. She is the best journalist and he is the best translator this earth has ever had. She has always been good to him as much as he had an eye for her. I am convinced that they will be a good match. Tell them that I am a bit disappointed but that I will always keep a place in my heart for them both. Make sure the team behaves in my absence and tell Baggy to try not to burn down the Delivery Drone's lab. Tell the security crew that they are the essence of the Anti-Bioterrorism and Biothreat Agency. Tell all the galls and guys that they are the trustworthy arms behind the A.B.B.A. principality. They'll know what it means. To you, Simon "Sam" Israël-Harding and to Lesley "Les" Douglass-Roken, I leave you both everything I own. All my possessions, fortune as well as my home belong to you now. Please take good care of my house, tend to my vegetable garden and take good care of Gaïus, my Argus monitor. You will find all the maintenance equipment necessary for the garden and the lizard's enclosure in the second shed, the one right behind the barn. I would have loved to be at your wedding and I would have loved to see your family grow successfully. All I can say is that I wish you both all the best. I love you both like my brothers and I will summon the most beautiful weather for your wedding from wherever I am. Always remember that your Warality resides in your ability to survive, to adapt and evolve to avoid and prevent extinction! This is the meaning of life.

Ps: Do me a favor. I want you to translate my research and send the final Waral code manuscript to Sister Odéna before you publish it. Sister Odéna still resides at the Sanctuary of the Chocolatine in New Gaul. She raised me after all. She is about to celebrate her one hundred and sixty-second birthday so you may have to wait a few seasons before you get any reply from her. She was always like a mother to me and I will always cherish her love. Make sure to tell her that."

Your old friend, Noël Joseph.